In memory of my father who instilled in many a love of Notre Dame
and with eternal thanks to my parents,
Margaret and Michael Dowling,
for following their faith
in the face of its fateful challenge

Published with the cooperation and support of the
University of Notre Dame Alumni Association
by MarySunshine Books, 1996
Design by E. Marten Schalm Jr.
Printing by World Wide Graphics, Bloomington, Indiana
Front cover photograph by Linda K. Dunn, taken two nights before Christmas,
    aided by the light of the nearby nativity scene
Back cover photograph by Richard L. Spicer in February 1981
Historical references from unpublished manuscript, "A Cave of Candles: The Story
    Behind the Notre Dame Grotto," Dorothy Corson Collection, University Archives

To submit your own story, to join these in the University Archives, write:
Grotto Stories, PO Box 454, Notre Dame, IN 46556-0454

ISBN 0-9652337-0-7

Photo taken from atop the Grotto as
Archbishop Agostino Cacciavillan,
Apostolic Pro-Nuncio to the U.S.,
commemorated the Grotto
centennial year on Lourdes Day,
February 11, 1996.

*"The Grotto is a place of faith. How
wonderful that Father Sorin and his
successors brought the spirit of Lourdes,
the spirit of Mary,
to the heartland, to inspire the prayers
of young people
for generations to come."*

*University President
Rev. Edward A. Malloy, C.S.C.,
at the Grotto's centennial commemoration.*

Between February the 11th and August the 16th of 1858, Bernadette Soubirous experienced eighteen separate visions of a "Lady" in the Grotto of Massabielle near the French town of Lourdes. This humble and guileless young woman, who did not know her catechism and could only recite the "Our Father" and the "Hail Mary," nonetheless stoutly withstood both the religious and the civil authorities of her day who challenged her account of the apparitions. "The Lady" requested prayers and religious processions, penance and deeper conversion, and the construction of a chapel at the Grotto. On March the 25th, Bernadette, at the insistence of her parish priest, asked "the Lady" who she was. The woman smiled and answered in the local dialect of that region: "Que soy Immaculada Councepciou" or "I am the Immaculate Conception." Bernadette said of herself: "I served the Blessed Virgin as a simple broom. When she no longer had any use for me, she put me back behind the door."

Father Basil Moreau, the founder of the congregation of Holy Cross, and Father Edward Sorin, the founder of the University of Notre Dame, both visited Lourdes on several occasions and both firmly believed in the miraculous nature of Bernadette's visions. In fact, the first organized pilgrimage to Lourdes from outside of France was led by Holy Cross priests from the University of Notre Dame. The earliest known representation of Our Lady of Lourdes in the United States can be seen in a stained glass window in the west transept of Notre Dame's Basilica of the Sacred Heart. It was always Father Sorin's fond desire to build a replica of the Lourdes Grotto at Our Lady's School. His dream was accomplished three years after his death when in 1896, Father Corby constructed and dedicated Notre Dame's Grotto.

Loving devotion for Mary is, of course, an ancient component of Catholic faith. Long before the writings of the New Testament were ever gathered into a single volume, Christians of both the East and the West honored Mary not only as the Mother of the Redeemer but also as the first and greatest of the Lord's disciples. In Catholic tradition, Mary is a symbol of the fidelity of ancient Israel and of the faith of the Church, the new "Israel of God." Mary was the first to receive Jesus Christ into her life. At her request, Jesus worked his first miracle in Cana of Galilee. Mary remained faithful, even at the foot of the cross. At the very birth of the Church on Pentecost Sunday, Mary was praying in the midst of the Apostles when they received the Holy Spirit. Now clothed in glory within the great Communion of Saints, Mary continues to pray with and for God's Church on earth.

Almost everyone who visits Notre Dame spends at least some time at the Grotto of Our Lady of Lourdes. For the last hundred years, nearly every student who has ever studied here has found the Grotto to be a place of welcome and prayer. Countless candles testify to the devotion of generations, all inspired by the loving witness of Mary. Here the Mother of Christ is deeply revered as the Blessed Mother of all those who believe in his Gospel and trust in the power of his grace. Hearts are comforted, lives are changed, and real miracles continue to happen. Faith is at the very heart of this University's life and mission, and the Grotto is at the very heart of Notre Dame.

REV. DANIEL R. JENKY, C.S.C.
RECTOR, BASILICA OF THE SACRED HEART
NOTRE DAME DU LAC
CLASS OF 1970

In the shadow of the Golden Dome,
tucked in a wooded hillside,
there is light.

A beacon of comfort for one
hundred years, the Grotto is
at the heart of Notre Dame.

At this rocky shrine to Mary,
the Mother of God,
in an idyllic lakeside setting,
lives are quietly touched.

Countless of the faithful have
brought their burdens and
their thanks to the Grotto,
lit a candle to prolong a prayer . . .
found peace.

Some of them have shared their
treasured memories.

Here are their words.

I was a cradle Domer, a child reared from infancy to attend Notre Dame. My father had attended Notre Dame for law school, and in my family's mind, South Bend was the Promised Land. My first words were "Go Irish." The Golden Dome has loomed before my eyes all my life. And when finally the time was upon me, I had been accepted (Notre Dame having thoughtfully gone co-ed when I was seven), my bags were packed (at least metaphorically speaking), I had only to attend to a last bit of paperwork — choosing a residence hall. I wanted Walsh, of course, with its warm yellow brick and bay windows, or Breen-Phillips or Farley, both of which had a certain North Quad charm and close proximity to the library and dining hall. Even a Pasquerilla East or West with their modern conveniences would do.

I did not want Lewis Hall. I had never heard of Lewis Hall, had never seen it that I knew of, despite my frequent trips to Notre Dame. The dorm I had been assigned was described as "architecturally straightforward," an ominous phrase if I'd ever heard one. It was a former convent. It was close to the lakes, which even a Southern girl knew meant cold winds, and close to St. Michael's Laundry which meant hot steam. Lewis Hall had nothing to offer.

Except the Grotto. Around the corner and slightly downhill from my architecturally straightforward nunnery was the lighted niche of the Grotto, a rocky reminder that Notre Dame means Our Lady, and that the undergraduate experience at Notre Dame is a lovely, everyday combination of the secular and the sacred.

I jogged the perimeter of the campus some winter nights, my lungs nearly frostbitten from the air I gasped in, and ended at the Grotto. I would kneel briefly at the iron railing and then climb stiffly up the hill to Lewis, having attended to body and soul. Passing by in the evenings, I could hear the murmur of the Rosary, said in all weather at 6:45 every night. The Grotto flamed particularly bright during exam week, of course, all that prayer made visible. To light a candle at the Grotto is to put your faith in faith, to believe that in our joy and sorrow there is some design, some Designer, who attends to our desires and fears. I was at Notre Dame the year the Grotto caught fire. I didn't know that stone could burn. But then again, maybe I did.

I saw a photograph once of the Grotto at Lourdes, the "real" Grotto, the owner of the photograph said. The only detail that distinguished the Lourdes Grotto from my Grotto was the row of crutches abandoned by those who came expecting miracles, demanding them even, and went away rejoicing. I suspect, though, that crutches have been shed too at the perhaps humbler Grotto in South Bend. I know that as I trudged off to struggle further with calculus, or to assume my position on the North Dining Hall slop line (a job description so gruesome that my mother forbade mention of it at the dinner table), to attend Mass at Sacred Heart or football at the stadium, that I was always conscious of the small warm flickers of light at my back.

We should add to the Irish blessing the following line: May the fires of Our Lady's Grotto always burn bright in your life.

MAURA MANDYCK
CLASS OF 1987
ATLANTA, GEORGIA

Shortly before 8 p.m. on December 1, 1969, I was the only one at the Grotto. It was a typical cold and windy South Bend evening, but nothing could have kept me away from the kneeler that night. It was the occasion of the first Vietnam War draft lottery, and for weeks I had been fearful that my birthday would be one of the first drawn. Several months before, I had registered with my local draft board as a "selective conscientious objector," meaning that I could not in good conscience participate in that war, although I did not claim to be a pacifist. However, draft boards all over the country were turning down such petitions, and if I got a low number in the lottery, I faced the prospect of going to jail.

I have to admit that, before that night, I had never been a "Grotto person." That was for my dad and uncles during nostalgic visits to the campus. But that night I was desperate enough to try anything, and, paradoxically, I prayed like a foxhole-bound combatant. I begged for the cup to pass, for Mary to assist me in the luck of the draw. "Please," I asked, "no low number for me. Let it be somebody else."

All of a sudden I heard a voice ask me, "Like who?"

Ever since that night I've wondered if that voice was within or without me. Of course, a skeptic would point out that it was grammatically incorrect, but I know that it spoke right to my condition, and left me stunned. After a few moments of collecting my composure, I was able to say, "O.K. Let it be me." I headed back to my room in Walsh Hall. As I opened my door the phone was ringing. It was one of my roommates calling from the library. "Are you O.K?" he asked. "I couldn't believe it when your birthday was the very first one drawn."

"I'm fine," I replied. "I'm really O.K." For the rest of the evening I fielded phone calls from relatives and friends, all of whom said that I was taking being number one in the draft lottery very well. A little over a year later, after many return visits to the Grotto, I managed to flunk my draft physical on St. Patrick's Day, thanks to a slight ailment I never thought would mean anything to me or the Army. But, by that time, I knew that I was being called not just to oppose a war, but to "wage peace" as we termed it in those days. I had decided that whatever I did in my life, I would try to live my conviction that all human life is precious and sacred.

Every time I hear the story of the marriage feast at Cana I am reminded that Mary changed her Son's life with only four words: "They have no wine."

I know how he must have felt. She changed mine with two.

GRIFF HOGAN
CLASS OF 1971
CINCINNATI, OHIO

The following is a poem I wrote during my first week of school freshman year at Notre Dame (published in the Fall 1994 *Juggler*). It is about a friend of mine who was killed by a car when we were twelve years old. The hundreds of dancing flames in the breezy August night mesmerized me and conjured up long-forgotten memories of my friend, Christopher Kelly. I will always remember this night at the Grotto when I finally found peace about his death and felt, I believe, Christopher at peace.

THE REBUKE OF THE SCHOLAR'S ANALYSIS OF THE GROTTO

And are those humble candles
Merely combustible fuels,
Chemical compositions,
And those praying merely fools?
And is that heat they release
Simple thermal energy,
Conservation of matter,
And fruitless humble pleas?
Is death and is suffering
The normal course of history,
Social law and necessity,
That the ignorant here don't see?
Is the stopping point of life
An ancient biofunction
An impersonal act of nature
Are the humble fools at this junction?

I have stared into the candle
Of one who is young and dead,
And saw him in that short candle,
Where life and death are wed.
I have spoken to the young one,
Who is gone, through the life-death flame,
And have rested on his restless soul,
Have been with him in life-death plane.
And for all your science, my friend,
You have no more answers than I;
Answers to things worth knowing;
Answers to the plain question "Why?"
I have no answers either,
Nor do any I suppose,
But I have faith my prayer reached him;
I think he the flickering flame blows.

As a crystal tear reflected
The shifting flame off my eye,
I saw the star that is his
Wink in the black, answerless sky.

DANIEL MURPHY
CLASS OF 1998
NOTRE DAME, INDIANA

Our son Ryan is now a junior at Notre Dame and often stops by the Grotto for a moment of quiet reflection, to say a prayer, or light a candle. On our trips to Notre Dame, we make a special point to stop by the Grotto to light a candle for our younger son, Brendan. Sadly, Brendan never got to see his brother go to Notre Dame. He died of cancer at age thirteen, when his brother was a junior in high school. But when I light a candle, somehow I know his spirit is there with us and that he watches over his brother. I know he would be so very proud of him.

Our own feelings about the Grotto are exemplified by the touching poem written by Dan Murphy, Class of '98, which was published in the fall, 1994, edition of Notre Dame's *The Juggler*. How well he shares our own yearning pain ... yet hope. Dan wrote the poem to find peace about the death of his own friend, Christopher Kelly, who died at the age of twelve. In writing it, he has helped bring us peace, too, especially when we light that candle at the Grotto for Brendan. Christopher, Brendan, and so many others ... they are all "bright stars winking in the black answerless sky." Thanks to Dan for sharing his poem.

JEAN MCMAHON
SOUTHBURY, CONNECTICUT

I have always loved the Grotto at any time of year, whether surrounded by the vibrant colors of fall, the white blanket of snow, or the new life of spring. In times of stress, pain, and joy, the sight of the candles glowing brightly gave me strength and faith. I knew that I was never alone because each candle represented someone else who was feeling the way I was.

The few times my family visited me on campus, we always stopped there to say a prayer and enjoy the time together. One of my favorite (and humorous) memories is the weekend of my graduation. My brother and a friend (whose sister was also graduating) were roaming the campus. They decided to stop by the Grotto, light a candle, and say a prayer for us. Coming from a high school freshman, this was one of the sweetest gestures he had ever done for me. My mother asked if he had given a donation for the candle. His face suddenly changed and he said, "Oh, you have to pay for the candles?" We stopped by the Grotto later that day, said a prayer, and gave a donation for the candles!

DIANE M. WAGROWSKI
CLASS OF 1994
BLOOMINGTON, INDIANA

I do not understand the power of prayer in its many forms; but I can attest to the fact that praying does get results, although not immediately and not always in ways that I had originally wanted. After all, God is not a cosmic wishing well. But I am convinced that prayers I brought to the Grotto when I was a student at Notre Dame have indeed been answered. I transferred to Notre Dame in 1978 from the University of Chicago and entered with advanced standing as a junior. I had declared pre-med at Chicago and was still stinging from the recommendation from my academic advisor there to give up my hopes for a career in medicine. She was concerned about my recovering body's ability to withstand the rigorous demands of the training process.

A month before I was to start college, I suffered a nearly fatal depressed fractured skull when I was struck in the head by the rotor blades of a helicopter, which were rotating at 4000 rpm. I remained comatose for 10 days. After awakening, the immediate consequences of the injury were a transient flaccid paralysis, a temporary partial amnesia, and an impairment of my coordination, agility, and reflexes — which contributed to a second brush with death between my first and second years of college. While I was working a summer construction job, a one-ton slab of concrete shifted from its perch seven feet above the ground and fell on me. I almost got out of the way, but not quite, resulting in fractures of my upper back and neck. A syndrome of easy fatigue and chronic pain was with me for the next 12 years.

Once at Notre Dame, I considered other majors, but I felt medicine calling me back at every turn. Father Walter, the pre-med advisor in charge of writing the cover letter of recommendation for all pre-meds at Notre Dame echoed the same discouraging advice I had received before leaving Chicago. I was in a quandary. The advice from those whose role it was to guide and counsel me was for me to quit pursuing my dream. In essence, I was told I could not cut it. But I felt I had to try. So, I put into God's hands the ultimate destiny of my academic journey and turned to Mary, the mother of Jesus, to be the guide and patroness of my studies. From 1978 until 1981, I joined Br. John Laville, Br. Beatus, Br. Cosmos, my Grotto buddy, Howard Horne, and a host of Notre Dame students and alumni in praying the 6:45 Rosary at the Grotto. Regardless of the weather, we gathered and recited in unison the centuries-old prayer which has such a deep but variable meaning for each of us.

At the Grotto, I asked for the wisdom to recognize and accept the new limits to my abilities. I sought the courage to persevere and the patience to overcome the effects of the two injuries. I also prayed to get into medical school. I initially applied to five medical schools. Two accepted me and I chose the University of Wisconsin, only to have my neck and back injuries flare up again during the winter of my first year. I struggled through medical school over 5+ years. During the difficulties of medical school, I had maintained my enthusiasm and passion for medicine by getting involved with global public health concerns through the Nobel Prize-winning International Physicians for the Prevention of Nuclear War. As graduation approached, however, I was feeling burned out and not ready to enter into a residency program for specialty training. At that time, I had heard about a graduate program at the new Institute for International Peace Studies on campus. I applied and was offered a fellowship in the MA program. So I took 18 months away from clinical training and returned to the land of Our Lady and the Grotto for some badly needed nurturance.

As a graduate student, I revisited the Grotto, where I had passed so much of my time as an undergraduate. There I was able to recenter myself on the teachings of Christ. I had left Notre Dame after earning my BA, afire with a disciple's zeal of service. During the traumatic process of medical school training, however, that zeal had gotten marginalized, devalued and displaced along the way. After completing my Master's degree, I returned to Madison for specialty training in Family Medicine. My solid spiritual foundation, rebuilt during that year under the Golden Dome and at the Grotto was about to be put to a test. During that first year of residency training, my frustration and despair began to mount regarding my slowness at "putting things together." I had suspected something was wrong as a graduate student at Notre Dame, but was too engaged with my studies to interrupt them to do anything about it. By means of some neuropsychologic testing and academic evaluation during my internship year, my intuition was confirmed when I was diagnosed as having residual dyslexia. For almost 17 years, as a result of coping, not excelling, my self-image and self-confidence had been crumbling. I realized only after I had received the diagnosis that the phantom I had been fighting all that time was not an inherent character flaw. The diagnosis of a learning disability allowed me to heal a badly bruised and battered sense of self-esteem.

Today, my shingle is hung almost in the shadow of the Golden Dome. I am a family physician in partnership with one of the most respected senior practitioners in the state. I long ago fully recovered physically from the two traumatic injuries. The residual dyslexia I look at now as a non-threatening occasional annoyance. I believe that the daily (well, almost) recitation of the Rosary at the Grotto as an undergraduate and my ongoing prayers to the Holy Spirit were just as important as all of my years of studying. In fact, prayer is how I received the fortitude to persevere.

I do not want to sound pie in the sky about my prayers at the Grotto — clearly, I know how hard I have worked and how much I have overcome to get to where I am today. But I brought myself in trust to the sacred and holy place of the Grotto and clearly experienced God's loving presence and guidance in answer to the prayer of my heart poured out at the Grotto. God looked upon me in my lowliness and brokenness and has had mercy. And I am so grateful.

FRANK M. CASTILLO, M.D.
CLASS OF 1981, 1990
SOUTH BEND, INDIANA

This happened to me in May of my freshman year at Notre Dame, 1941. I was praying at the Grotto, and I was feeling pretty low because a friend of mine had passed away. This friend and I had been together through grammar school, high school, and we came up to Notre Dame together. We were to room together in Badin Hall our sophomore year.

As I knelt praying, my state of mind must have been apparent because an elderly Holy Cross nun came over to where I was kneeling, put her hand on my shoulder and said, "She will never let you down." From that moment the sun shone, and my gloom was gone. Even today, after fifty years, I get a chill when I think of her words. You know, Sister was right. Mary (through Her Son) has never let me down.

When I visit Notre Dame, my first stop is at the Grotto, thanking Mary and Her Son for getting me back, and my last stop at Notre Dame is the Grotto, asking Her to let me return to Notre Dame again someday.

VICTOR S. COLLETTI
CLASS OF 1944
PORT ARTHUR, TEXAS

REV. JOHN E. FITZGERALD wrote in the *Scholastic*, May 2, 1950:

"From the great Golden Dome of her University, Our Lady reigns as our Queen. Yet at the Grotto, she seems to have stepped down a little closer to us that she might emphasize the other side of her personal relationship with us — that of Our Mother."

Although it has been over forty years since I graduated from Notre Dame, I have never forgotten the Grotto. I remember so many visits there (especially before exams) and the spiritual comfort it afforded me — as well as so many thousands of others. That is why, in my will, I have bequeathed $150,000 for the building of a Grotto exactly like the one at Notre Dame and an additional $50,000 in trust for its maintenance to a small Catholic college here in New England. It gives me great pleasure to know that for many generations to come, students at this small school will have a visual reminder of the Blessed Mother and will look to her for comfort and inspiration. I have ordered a plaque to be placed at the Grotto to read "In loving memory of my parents." Wouldn't it be terrific if many of the Catholic schools in the United States had a "Notre Dame Grotto!"

ANONYMOUS

I remember the May evenings when our group from the dining table paraded to the Grotto to sing hymns to the Blessed Mother. I remember most Father Steiner urging the assembled students to belt out, "Macula non est in te." Later, I led my two daughters at our May altar, trying to sing the hymns, but especially, "Macula non est in te."

BILL ROCKENSTEIN
CLASS OF 1934
WHEELING, WEST VIRGINIA

In 1984, I took my daughter to visit Notre Dame when she was a junior in high school. Of course, she fell in love with Notre Dame. Many times that weekend I visited the Grotto, just in awe and full of hope. Before leaving I remember asking the Virgin Mother at the Grotto if it was to be for my daughter to be accepted at Notre Dame, to help me find a way to make the dream come true. Mary Jo was accepted. God provided the means and she graduated in 1990.

In 1988, my wife was very ill. We had a daughter at Notre Dame and a daughter at The University of Dayton and still two more children at home. I needed help. I went to the Grotto; I asked for help. My wife started to get better. The doctor prescribed medication that brought my wife and our life back to all of us.

In the fall of 1994, my grand-nephew Sean was diagnosed as having Terrettz disease. I have a great belief in the St. Maurice blessing. It is a Benedictine blessing given to the patient. I made arrangements for this blessing to be given to Sean, but I still wanted to get to my Grotto. Marilyn and I went to visit the Grotto over Thanksgiving. We arrived in time to say the Rosary with the group, and I asked for help for my nephew who was so young and so perfect. Please spare him. Sean no longer has spasms, and it is believed he will be off all medication very soon.

In 1993, I lost my job, the term is down-sizing. I struggled with different situations and tried to make many things work to no avail. In April of 1995, I went to the Grotto to pray for help. I still have two girls in college, one at Marquette University and one starting Xavier University. On May 8th, I started a new job with a very fine future for myself and my family. I only hope that I never become too old or feeble that I am unable to visit my Grotto.

JOE FOGERTY
WEST CHESTER, OHIO

THE MOTHER of Lt. Lawrence A. Barrett, graduate cum laude of the Class of 1940, wrote a remembrance of him after his death in a plane crash during World War II. Her letter was published in the May 12, 1944, *Scholastic*: "How glad I am that Larry had those happy years at Notre Dame. He carried from there his habit of living his faith; if ever a boy used his religion, he did, with all his heart, as he did everything. I have a comforting little belief that on May evenings when the boys are at the Grotto, his dear voice rises again ... 'Macula non est in te' ... such a host of her Notre Dame boys are even nearer to her now, young and fine forever."

Inscriptions in the circular candle tiers at the Grotto and the black arm rest at the kneeler read: "In Memorial to Paul Purcell, 1943." Purcell, Class of 1940, died in a stateside airplane crash.

Margaret '92 and Tom Clare '92, '95JD
May 22, 1993

I was a 1939 fall freshman at ND. Midterm of my Junior year, January 1942, I enlisted in the Army Corps. I completed pilot training, and went in the Air Corps and became the pilot of a B-17, flying combat missions out of England in late 1943. On December 30, 1943, our B-17 was shot down by the German Air Force and I became an "Envader" in the French Underground! My parents were informed that I was missing in action. In early February my mother went to South Bend to visit a rather serious girlfriend that I had, and that my mother knew and liked, as well as her parents. On the 1st or 2nd of February, Ruth and my mother made a very lengthy visit to the Grotto and then returned to Ruth's home. When they arrived back at Ruth's home, my father had just called to inform my mother that I had just safely returned for duty to my Air Force Base in England. Through all the years my mom and dad were convinced that the time spent in the Grotto by my mom had paid them the Big Dividends, and had returned me safely to the land of the living.

RICHARD M. SMITH
CLASS OF 1943, 1947
BATTLE LAKE, MINNESOTA

After receiving my diploma I asked Therese to walk to the Grotto and say a prayer, my sister Ellie asked if she could come with us and Therese said "sure." So off we went and there sat a priest on a bench. We talked for a while and he asked if we were engaged. Therese said she had a Notre Dame miniature and I said "Yes, we are" and put the ring on her finger and the priest blessed it. I could not have planned it better. We have always made it a point to stop at the Grotto whenever we are on campus. We have five children and twelve grandchildren. Our son, Michael, became engaged to Julie Kanak at the Grotto while he was a student eleven years ago. They have four sons.

ROBERT J. RIGALI
CLASS OF 1954
NILES, ILLINOIS

As a graduate student attending summer sessions in 1968, I would jog in the early evening from the center of campus to St. Mary's and back, finishing at the Grotto, where there was a drinking fountain. Even though the water was tepid, it was welcome after the run. Having slaked my temporal thirst, I would kneel for a few minutes in attempt to satisfy my spiritual needs. I would ask the Blessed Mother to intercede with her Divine Son on my behalf in such life shaping matters as passing my orals and my date with Army induction after graduation. For after all, with graduation I would enter the select group of Notre Dame men who could count themselves as being special sons of Mary.

In the following twenty-five years, no annual pilgrimage to Notre Dame was complete without a stop at the Grotto to light a candle and to request of the Blessed Mother some special intercession for a need that was paramount at that time. In 1993, my family hosted a gracious young lady of fifteen from Northern Ireland as part of the Ulster Project. The Ulster Project is a program for bringing Catholic and Protestant teenagers from strife-torn Northern Ireland to the United States for a month of intense interactivity in an attempt to show them that they can live together in peace as Catholics and Protestants do in the United States.

One weekend we took her on a tour of Ohio and Indiana so that she could see the geography and culture of the Midwest. Naturally, we had to stop at Notre Dame. She was awed by the Golden Dome, impressed by Sacred Heart Church, and thrilled by ducklings in the library reflection pool. She compared the architecture of the south quad to the buildings of Cambridge College in England where her sister was a student and politely listened to my stories of Fair Catch Corby, Number One Moses and Touchdown Jesus.

After finishing the grand tour, we sat enjoying one of her favorite American foods, ice cream, and I asked her what impressed her most about Notre Dame. She said she had never seen men kneeling in prayer in public as she had observed at the Grotto. It was just not done in Northern Ireland. She marveled at what would motivate men to display their faith in public and remarked that there must be something special about this Grotto place and the men who frequented it.

The Irish lassie understood after only a few hours what innumerable Notre Dame men have come to learn in their hearts — Notre Dame is special, and Notre Dame men are special because of Notre Dame. That specialty comes not from the buildings, the greenery of the campus, the intellectual discipline of the classroom, nor the football tradition, but from faith in and love of God and the love returned by that God, and faith that "no matter what the odds be great or small" the Mother of God will be there to comfort her sons of Notre Dame.

JOHN G. ADORJAN
1968 M.A.
PICKERINGTON, OHIO

THE THREE-SIDED sculptured drinking fountain at the Grotto depicts Jesus at the well; preaching from the boat; and washing the feet of his disciples. The fountain — the work of sculptor John Schickel — stands at the spot where builders struck a natural spring during construction of the Grotto. The water emerged in the same vicinity relative to the Grotto as it had at Lourdes.

The attraction of the spring was noted August 22, 1896 in *The Kalamazoo Augustinian* description of an early pilgrimage from that city to Notre Dame: "The Grotto was a beautiful surprise. Although much had been promised, more than what was promised was realized. It is a wonderful creation. It was the favorite spot for the pilgrims throughout the day. The spring was tested and more than one favor was received. It was a day of joy, peace, devotion and happiness long to be remembered. Gallons of water from the spring were carried away."

During senior parents weekend, my husband and I were with our son, Kevin, at the Grotto. It was two o'clock in the morning. Snow and ice covered the ground, and it was so very cold. The three of us were huddled together, shivering on a bench while watching all those candles and vigil lights burning, dancing and glowing brightly. Kevin's eyes welled up, and with a broken voice he said he didn't know what he would do if anything ever happened to us or how to thank us. Finally, he just said, "I love you both so much." When we make our annual visit to Notre Dame and the Grotto we relive the moment, cry a little and feel warm all over.

K.I.S.

This little Grotto story takes place in June, 1995, while my husband, Jim, and I attended our fourth Notre Dame Elderhostel. One afternoon I rode a bike down to the Grotto, sat on a bench in the sun and just looked around. I drank in the whole Grotto scene slowly and languishingly with special attention to the candles ... the candles; what was on the minds of those persons who knelt before them, what was in their hearts? How many boys and girls, men and women laid out their souls, opened their hearts and minds in that sacred oasis? I began to think of the previous times I had been to the Grotto and where I was in my life at those times, reflecting back further and further. I was feeling quite melancholy, pondering the seemingly lost years, my eyes resting on the young people passing by. Here I was, all at once an elderhosteler. When did it all happen?

Down the path from the street came a young mother pushing a sleeping baby in a stroller with three older children. She sat on a bench in the shade with her sleeping baby and with her head resting on her hand, watched as her kids marched with assurance directly into the Grotto, behind the railing and ceremoniously lit every candle in the whole place.

How I yearned to be a young mother again. Yearning and desire gripped my heart. I wanted to be able to sit there with my young babies and to relive a moment I hadn't thought about in 30 years. It was in the early sixties when so many of us young parents had a bunch of kids and no money. We lived very sparingly. We never went anywhere, not even fast foods. But because we loved Notre Dame so much and Jim being a subway alumnus big time, we got tickets to a Blue-Gold game in the spring, two bucks a ticket. It was the BIG event for us.

The long-anticipated Saturday arrived and we loaded the rusty, yellow station wagon with the stroller, playpen, lunches, Kool Aid, etc. It was a beautiful day and each one of us together ended up down at the Grotto. Daddy read the letter from Tom Dooley and explained all the Grotto stuff. As I picture it now, we must have been quite a sight, all kneeling in a row praying and whispering.

The kids asked, "Mommy, can we light a candle?"

"Do you think money grows on trees? If I let one of you light a candle, I'd have to let all of you light a candle."

"Please, Mommy?"

"No," I said. "Aren't you kids ever satisfied?" I probably said all that kind of stuff and remembering that moment now nearly tore me apart with regret and desire. Tears were burning holes in my cheeks. I could hardly breathe. I left the Grotto. I couldn't cope. I had to walk my bike back to Lewis Hall because I couldn't see where I was going, so blurred was my vision from crying. I tried some centering exercises that helped but I still wished I had let the kids light a candle.

A few days later I rode my bike down to the Grotto again. This time I sat on a bench in the shade and tried some more contemplation. When I opened my eyes, I saw two small roly-poly boys and their mother behind them. It was very hot and the boys were wiping the sweat from their faces with their black T-shirts. Mother, too, dressed all in black, was very hot and agitated. She had on thongs and her hair was pulled tightly back in a rubber band, wet with perspiration. You could tell this was her first time at the Grotto and upon scanning all the people praying and the obvious reverence, felt a little self-conscious.

"Shhhh," she scolded her boys and kind of pushed and pulled at them. She forced them to a kneeling position at the railing and pulled out from a net bag a small camera. It was awkward for her to try to get the Grotto in the background and them kneeling and facing the camera at the same time.

I went up to her and said, "If you'd like, I could take a picture of you all together."

"That would be nice," she said. "Where should we stand?"

"I have an idea," I said. "Why don't you stand behind the altar? There is a big ND insignia in front of the altar and the boys could pretend they're saying Mass. It always makes for a good picture."

She and her boys did just that and I took the picture. She came down from the altar and thanked me. I gave her the camera. She looked at me. Her boys looked up at me. Her boys looked up at her. She looked down at her boys. The expression on her face softened. She hesitated. Then she turned to me and said very innocently, "Can we light a candle?"

I said, "Yes."

It was a profound experience for me because it made me reflect. I came to the realization that I was all those mothers. I was the first mother who let her children light all the candles. I was the second mother who said, "No." I was the third mother who asked, and I was the fourth mother who said, "Yes."

We are all mothers. This experience transcended time for me.

MARY MURPHY
OAK LAWN, ILLINOIS

This 1992 photo of Dennis Kinney was printed in Shaped By Images, *by Episcopal minister Rev. Seth Adams. It appeared in the chapter titled, "One Who Keeps Rituals."*

"And thus my grandson became a part of the Grotto's shared significance with another religion and its teachings," wrote Robert Kinney, Class of 1947.

Although not terribly fascinating or unbelievable, my Grotto story provides a lasting memory of my Notre Dame experience. From the very day I arrived on the ND campus as an awkward freshman in late August of 1984 until my graduation on May 13, 1988, I visited and prayed at the grotto each and every day. Regardless of weather, engineering exams, sporting events, SYRs, or whatever, I made the trek from the library or Grace Hall to the Grotto each night.

I always found solace when quietly praying at the Grotto. I remember lighting a few candles during my four years at ND: one when my best friend's little brother died of Muscular Dystrophy, and a couple of others for special intentions. Praying at the Grotto allowed me to put everything in perspective and offered a subtle yet powerful reminder that God was always there, listening to me.

The Grotto was the last place I stopped at before departing from the campus after my graduation ceremony. It is the one physical place that I miss most, and the first place I will visit when I return to the ND campus.

CHRISTOPHER ALLEN
CLASS OF 1988
ESCONDIDO, CALIFORNIA

As a daily ritual after dinner at the South Dining Hall, my friends from Cavanaugh Hall and I would always go back to the dorm by the way of the Grotto for a short visit. One late winter evening in 1955, as we approached the Grotto, we heard cries of help from an older classmate who had fallen through the ice on Lake St. Mary. We successfully pulled the student out of the lake. He was frozen, but safe. Besides remembering his soggy daily Missal, I can still visualize his face even though I still don't know his name. Maybe he would have been rescued by someone else, but I'm sure our daily visit to the Grotto had something to do with it.

With love always for Notre Dame and for all she stands,

MICHAEL M. MADDEN, M.D.
CLASS OF 1958
BUFFALO, NEW YORK

From Scholastic, *September 8, 1888*

"Probably the largest representation of the apparition of Our Lady of Lourdes that exists anywhere was lately finished by Signor Gregori in a Gothic angle of the church of the Sacred Heart at Notre Dame over an altar dedicated to the Immaculate Conception. It represents the fifth apparition. The Blessed Virgin stands over a cleft of the rock; the rosary is suspended on her wrist, and she is about to make the Sign of the Cross. Bernadette kneels at her feet, gazing upward and holding a lighted taper. The stream in the foreground, the rocks and foliage are skillfully painted, and so true to nature as to deceive those entering the church at the main door. The painting is 12 feet wide below and twice as high."

The Grotto painting remains in the Basilica, although the Lourdes altar under the painting was removed during one of the renovations.

I am a 1978 St. Mary's graduate and my husband is a 1977 Notre Dame graduate. Except for two years in Ireland, we have lived in Tennessee since we both graduated. We have made it a habit to go back to South Bend at least once a year. There is something very wonderful about ND/SMC campuses and the Grotto is the most spiritual place anywhere. I spent much time there during my college days, as did my friends. It is where we would go to think, to pray and work out our problems. I remember my sophomore year one of my roommates just found out her dad was diagnosed with lung cancer. We went to the Grotto, lit a candle, and said a prayer and I gave her my St. Jude Medal. His cancer was eventually cured.

The Grotto is always one of my first stops when we arrive. I usually have a list of people that want me to light candles for them, people who have never been to the Grotto, but have heard about it. I love the Grotto during the day, at night, covered with snow, in the fall with all the brightly colored leaves. One of my favorite sights is after a football game when it is dusk and seeing all those candles, too many for holders, just illuminating the Grotto. We are bringing our kids to a football game this year. Even though they have been to Bowl games, they have never been on campus. They have heard me talk about the Grotto and seen pictures of it. They can't wait to see it as I can't wait to show them. The Grotto represents the spirit of the Notre Dame family.

ANNETTE J. HAYDEN
BRENTWOOD, TENNESSEE

I graduated from Notre Dame in 1994 and I can honestly say that praying at the Grotto got me through the tough times and made the good times even better. There is no other place in the world where I can feel Mary's presence quite so strongly. I did not really know the Blessed Mother until I came to Notre Dame. At first I prayed to her there simply because it was expected. But she reached out to me, as she does to everyone, and truly spoke to my mind and heart. Now, I'm not saying I ever heard a physical inner or outer voice, but I began to hear her loving wisdom in my thoughts. I would be down there on my knees, sobbing over something like a crush I had on a guy who didn't notice or want my affections. And suddenly I'd think, "That's okay, because a wonderful man will come along for you someday." I eventually realized that these thoughts of optimism and hope were Mary's way of speaking to me. And so I would go there and pray to her when I felt sad or stressed or angry and she would bring me strength and comfort, time and time and time again. I pray to her here in Pittsburgh, but it's just not the same. There are no lakes or candles or benches or flowers surrounding me here as there are at the Grotto. It may sound strange but at the Grotto, after praying for a while, my breathing would change ... my breaths became strangely smooth and rhythmic and soothing. I really can't explain it, but I can say that when it happened I knew Mary was with me, surrounding me, loving me and I felt an incredible peace.

She is everywhere, of course. But somehow that Grotto is different. The place embodies the miracle of the Blessed Mother and its aura emanates her beautiful, loving presence. I feel forever blessed to have experienced that holy, holy place.

NANCY STUDNICKI
CLASS OF 1994
PITTSBURGH, PENNSYLVANIA

"Rev. Daniel Jenky, C.S.C. described the Grotto as a place where 'even non-church-goers feel they can go to be quiet and pray.'
He noted the reaction of a visiting Canadian priest to the enormous numbers of students who came to the Grotto to pray.
'At Notre Dame, there is still the atmosphere that gives people permission to pray without looking like they're doing anything weird.'"
From The Observer, February 13, 1986

During my first visit to Notre Dame, guided by my brother's brother-in-law, Tim Jordan (Class of 1974), I realized that no graduate ever leaves Notre Dame without being impacted by the peace, spirit and inspiration of the Grotto. For me, there are three memorable events where the Grotto positively impacted my life. It was where I: Learned the significance of prayer; passed on the importance of play; and proposed an everlasting bond of love.

As a walk-on freshman kicker for the varsity football team, the upper class kickers would always drag me to the Grotto after our nightly team meetings. Hardly an evening passed when Harry Oliver and Mike Johnston did not stop by the Grotto after the meetings to say a few prayers. I admired their faith and devotion and that became an inspiration for me. After a while it seemed unnatural not to stop by the Grotto after our team meetings.

As a resident assistant in Alumni Hall I was lucky to be assigned to the infamous freshmen alley on the first floor. I got my share of pranks played on me, including having my entire room placed out on the South Quad, door included. One night, after what I am sure was some long hours of devoted study time by all the freshmen in the alley, I invited the birthday boy, John Nickodemus, to reflect on turning 18 with me at the Grotto. Unbeknownst to him, I invited the rest of the alley to hide in trees and bushes near the Grotto. After we finished our prayers and started walking away, dark figures appeared and grabbed John and carried him, kicking and screaming, to a resting place in the nearby lake. Fortunately, we had someone bring a blanket for him.

Not having gone to Notre Dame, my girlfriend, but soon to be fiance, did not realize the importance of the Grotto. So one weekend I convinced her to go to South Bend from Chicago to visit some of my college friends who were there for a wedding. It did not make sense to her, since we saw them the night before, but I had to get her to the Grotto somehow to ask her to be my wife. When we finally made it to the Grotto, I was relieved to find very few people present, since I wanted to propose in private and have a natural, memorable moment together. As we knelt down to pray, I heard a golf cart pull up behind us. Much to my dismay, it was time for a very slow walking Brother to clean the wax from the candle holders and to fill in all of the empty candle slots. Each trip back to the golf cart I was hoping was his last. My wife's knees got so sore kneeling that she went back to sit down. A few minutes later, I followed her and we sat for some time in silence, me waiting for the brother to complete his task. It must have been 40 minutes later when he was finally driving off. Immediately, but not wanting to appear too anxious or nervous, we lit candles for our parents as I proposed. It was a truly memorable moment, and she even said "yes." Afterwards, we attended Mass at Sacred Heart and there, coincidentally, ran into the person who first introduced me to the Grotto, Tim Jordan.

GARY M. PURK
CLASS OF 1984
LAGRANGE, ILLINOIS

My story of the Notre Dame Grotto goes back to a time when I was 10 years old. At the time, my parents were visiting Notre Dame for the annual convention of Christian Family Movement. A night procession to the Grotto was planned for participants. I had never seen anything like it. Hundreds and hundreds of flickering candle flames dotted the circle around Saint Mary's lake, as the procession moved toward the Grotto. It was a moment I still recall 37 years later. At that time, my parents were still married, and we lived in Toledo, Ohio. Sighting the Golden Dome, which glinted with the last slanting rays of the late afternoon sun, we knew our long drive was over. Soon after we got settled into Keenan Hall, with its dark military green lockers and metal bunks, the gathering began for the candlelight procession. When the weekend ended, I prayed out loud, "I hope I live there someday."

For going on 23 years, it just happens that I have lived here, in the shadow of the Golden Dome, within hiking distance of that special Grotto I visited so long ago when I was a child. And now I bring my grandchild.

My second Grotto story is about a woman I thought I could never like who became so dear to us that she was like a grandmother to our children by the time she died, and the Grotto had a place in our relationship.

The woman had lived across the street from us for several years when we first had a personal conversation with her. It's not that we didn't try. She was just a little hard to get to know. And I wasn't sure I even wanted to get to know her. The few times I saw her, she was very angry and was taking her broom after neighborhood children who rang her doorbell and ran off. The image of this feisty little woman chasing small children with a broom makes me chuckle now, but then it made me want to leave her alone.

One day when I was on campus for an errand, a heavy downpour had begun, when suddenly my neighbor passed alongside my car, running briskly. I slowed down, cranked down my window and asked "Mrs. Feisty" if she wanted a ride. To my surprise, she answered "yes." We made small talk, and I dropped her off and forgot the incident. Soon after, a parish program turned up the fact that Mrs. Feisty had been a Catholic at one time. After some talks with our pastor, she returned to the Church after 31 years away. She was overjoyed to return to the faith of her mother, who was Catholic. We took Mrs. Feisty under our wing and brought her to Sunday Mass each week. On one occasion, I also brought her to Notre Dame to the Grotto. She moved slowly, cautiously, toward a darkened stone to the right and reverently stroked it. Then she told me it was the stone from the original Grotto at Lourdes. It was a moving moment, watching her fall in love with her Catholic faith all over again. I am reminded now of the saying, "How it improves people for us when we begin to love them."

TWO BLACK STONES, brought from visits to the Lourdes Grotto in France, were cemented into the Notre Dame Grotto. The larger relic was brought back by Rev. Joseph Maguire in 1958; the smaller by Rev. John F. DeGroote in 1939.

KATHLEEN FERRONE
SOUTH BEND, INDIANA

It was nearly 6 p.m. on December 23, 1991, when we walked up to the Grotto. I have heard stories of this happening to others, but I had no idea just then what was about to happen to me! I graduated from Saint Mary's College in 1986 and started dating David two years later while living and working in Detroit. David went to graduate school at Notre Dame, where he received his MBA in 1991. It was during his two years in the MBA program that we both formed a special bond with Notre Dame.

Earlier in the day we drove from near Detroit to Marshall, Michigan, to visit the Christmas shops in the quaint village. In mid-afternoon, David suggested that we drive to Notre Dame to look at the Christmas lights on campus. After years of driving long distances to see one another, the additional one-and-a-half-hour drive from Marshall did not seem like much.

Just as we approached the Grotto, as if by divine intervention, the Christmas lights turned on in a flash of brilliance. While kneeling at the rail after saying a prayer, a bird began chirping behind us, then stopped. He chirped again and David said, "Look! Over there!" I turned to look, but did not see anything. When I turned back, I could not believe my eyes! Sitting on the rail in front of me was an open box containing a diamond ring! At that moment, David asked, "Will you marry me?" I jumped up and began crying and hugged and kissed him! I almost forgot to say "yes", but I did. We then lit a votive candle and said a prayer. We were married on June 19, 1993. Every chance we get, we return to the Grotto to remember our special day!

JOANNE DELOREY WALKOWSKI
PHOENIX, ARIZONA

In 1976, my wife and I met at the Grotto. Sue was a student at St. Mary's College, and I was a law student at Notre Dame. We did not know each other. On a bright, sunny day in September, each of us fortuitously visited the Grotto, trying to find peace and solitude after a long day of classes. As it turned out, we found each other and were married the following year!

It is now 19 years and three children later. We thank God and the Blessed Mother for the gifts they have bestowed on our marriage and on our children. And we thank them for the Grotto memories that we'll always cherish. For us, the Grotto is a constant reminder that God truly exists, and that He is intimately involved in our daily lives.

CHRIS LOOMIS
CLASS OF 1979 J.D.
YARDLEY, PENNSYLVANIA

No story to enlighten; no miracle to be told. Yet, a picture embedded into my mind and soul and heart. That picture became a photo. That photo became my personal icon. In Henri J.M. Nouwen's book *Behold the Beauty of the Lord: Praying with Icons*, he says, "During a hard period of my life in which verbal prayer had become nearly impossible and during which mental and emotional fatigue had made me the easy victim of feelings of despair and fear, this icon became the beginning of my healing. As I sat for long hours in front of Rublev's Trinity, I noticed how gradually my gaze became prayer. This silent prayer slowly made my inner restlessness melt away and lifted me up into the circle of love, a circle that couldn't be broken by the powers of the world. Even as I moved away from the icon and became involved in the many tasks of everyday life, I felt as if I did not have to leave the holy place I had found and could dwell there wherever I went. I knew that the house of love I had entered has no boundaries and embraces everyone who wants to dwell there."

Now 13 years since graduating from ND, far from the Grotto, I pull out my photo of the statue of Mary, look at it, and it brings me back to the Grotto, to Mary Jo, to within, to beyond, to a place no longer defined — my icon. I gave the photo as gifts to most of my fellow Badinites and my boyfriend from Sorin. Years later when I graduated from dental school, I heard that my close friend, Mary Jo Mahaney, was in a coma from a car wreck. All I had was memories of her smile, our pizza and coke runs at 11 p.m. and her spirit. Five years later, she died. During that time, I would write not knowing if she could hear her mother's words. I often think of Mrs. Mahaney. What to do or say? Send the photo. The Grotto became alive with color and passion because once I shared with Mary Jo her love for Notre Dame. "In the world you will have trouble. But be brave: I have conquered the world." *JN Bible*

JENNIFER JONES
CLASS OF 1982
SEATTLE, WASHINGTON

Jennifer Jones is also the name of the actress who won an Academy Award for her performance in "The Song of Bernadette," the 1943 movie based on the experiences of Bernadette Soubirous at the Lourdes Grotto in France. It was her first movie. The film also won best cinema photography, best interior decoration and best score. George Seaton's script was nominated for best screenplay.

When I was a small child, my father was sent to Vietnam to participate in the Vietnam War. My mother, who was from South Bend, returned here with my sister and I to live with her parents while my father was at war. My grandfather, Paul Sergio, owned the shoe shop on the campus of Notre Dame for twenty-five years (the shoe shop is now the Copy Center). I would oftentimes go to work with my grandfather, and when I did he would take me to the Grotto at lunch time to light candles and pray. Even as a small child, I could feel something special and powerful about the Grotto; there was something awe-inspiring about it for me even then. We lit candles for the safe return of my father, for family we had lost, and I grew to love the Grotto. My father returned home safely from Vietnam and shortly thereafter, my grandfather died. After my grandfather died, the Grotto held an even more precious place in my heart. When my father returned from the war, we talked of the Grotto, and he told me that he had gone there often when he was a student at Notre Dame. Last year I moved my family from Texas to South Bend to take a job at Notre Dame. Since that time when I shared the Grotto with my grandfather, I have been drawn to Notre Dame and to the Grotto. I have always wanted to come back here. One of the first things I did was share it with my own two daughters, and we frequently visit it to light candles for my father, who died from Agent Orange related cancer, and my grandfather. It's like touching them both again, knowing that my father had prayed there many times himself, and that my grandfather loved it as well. Notre Dame and the Grotto are such a strong part of my family history; it is a joy for me to be able to pass it along and share it with my children knowing that when they grow up, they will have their own special memories of both places.

PAULA MUHLHERR ASHLEY
SOUTH BEND, INDIANA

My mother was a life-long Notre Dame fan, and I eagerly awaited her visit in October of my sopho-more year. We went to Mass at Sacred Heart — and we lit a candle together at the Grotto. In November, I returned to the Grotto, but this time I lit a candle alone. I had just learned that my mother was dying, and there was only one place I wanted to be. The Grotto is my spiritual home, where I feel closest to God — His benevolence, His mercy, and His love. And now it is where I feel closest to my mother.

DANIEL C. GAMACHE
CLASS OF 1988
LONG LAKE, MINNESOTA

It was not easy being a student at Notre Dame. Besides being legally blind, I was one of only a few Episcopalians on campus at the time. I was fortunate, however, to be at Notre Dame at a time when there were three Episcopalians on the faculty. Without these wonderful people, as well as my student friends, I would have felt very isolated indeed.

To paraphrase St. Paul in I Cor. 13, I see the world "through glasses darkly"; not blind, but not fully sighted either. While I cannot read print at a distance, I can see lights — bright stars, Christmas lights, city lights, and especially candles. It was the candles as much as the story and spirituality of the Grotto that attracted me. I came often to light a candle and pray — in summer after Evensong and in winter in late afternoon or after dinner, to celebrate times of joy in academic or spiritual discovery, and in times of sadness and frustration, as when my Episcopalian mentors on the faculty did not receive tenure.

One thing I remember is that sometime between 1976 and 1978 the Grotto seemed to be neglected. Candles were not kept stocked and the place looked forsaken. Perhaps this was only a winter-time hiatus, but at that time, the Grotto seemed a dark and lonely place.

Two years ago I returned to take a course on the Psalms and a course on Anglicanism from George Carey, Archbishop of Canterbury. It was an extraordinary experience to meet and hear the person we Episcopalians look to with enormous respect, though he has no jurisdiction. He seemed delighted to be at Notre Dame. Perhaps that was because no one would think to look for him there! During that time I visited the Grotto again and found it restored, with more people than I ever remembered coming there to pray. It was wonderful to light a candle again. I hope to return this summer for another course from Archbishop Carey, and to make another pilgrimage to the Grotto to pray in thanksgiving for the place and heritage that is Notre Dame — and for the unity of Christians.

JAN ROBITSCHER 1978 M.A.
BERKELEY, CALIFORNIA

"A young couple, he a Notre Dame graduate, visiting the Grotto told a Brother who was working there that they had tried unsuccessfully to have children. They asked the Brother to pray for them and to light a candle at the Grotto for this intention. Some years later they returned to the Grotto, this time with four lovely youngsters and another on the way. After praying in gratitude to Our Lady, they thanked the Brother for his prayers and added: 'But, please blow out the candle!'"

Brother James Lakofka, C.S.C., director of Lourdes Confraternity, quoted in Province Review, *April 1996*

FROM THE 1916 *Dome*

SECLUDED SPOT WHEREIN THE VERY AIR, WHISPERS AMONG THE TREES A VESPER PRAYER.

When I was an off-campus student at Notre Dame, 1924 to 1928, I had a free room at an undertaker's establishment, the A.M. Russell Funeral Chapel. My roommate was another student, Earl J. Dardes, who came from Titusville, Pennsylvania. We answered telephone calls at night and sometimes went on ambulance calls or drove a small van called "The Black Mariah" to one of the hospitals to pick up bodies.

We also worked at restaurants where we got our meals but did not eat breakfast there because we fasted for daily Communion at Father John O'Hara's chapel in Sorin Hall at N.D. We took turns buying day-old rolls or doughnuts at a bakery and shared them after our first class when we met at the Grotto for a brief visit and sip from the drinking fountain there. As we neared the end of our senior year we thought we should leave some mark of our daily visits, so we pried up a large rock at one side of the north stairway to the Grotto to each put a penny and a seven-cent streetcar token under it. After graduation, Earl left for home in Titusville while I stayed for a job at *The South Bend News-Times*. I got back to the campus occasionally, but it was years before Earl stopped by while on a cross-country trip. We went out to the University together and stopped at the Grotto to look for the rock under which we had left the pennies, but could not tell which one it was. Earl died a year or so later. I often stop at the Grotto and wonder if the coins are still there but would not disturb them if I knew, since they are a memorial to our daily visits as students.

I visited Earl in Titusville in 1936 and while there met his cousin, Evelu C. Seyboldt. Two years later, she became my wife. We have four sons.

GEORGE SCHEUER
CLASS OF 1928
SOUTH BEND, INDIANA

"The Grotto"
Junior Year, 1991
(Given to my father 29 years after he graduated from
Notre Dame and one year before I did).

The little flames dance in my eyes
as I kneel down, wrapping my body together
and away from the biting wind.

As I come to this amazing place,
my mind thinks of all those ghosts
whose prayers mingle with the holy air.

I pray for my father, who was once a son,
who came seeking solace, or to pray for his mother.

I wonder what he thought about,
braving these same winter nights
to offer words to heaven here.

I pray for the prayers he had,
which are manifest in his children's visions,
their hearts and their dreams.

I pray for my dreams.
May they bring me closer to Christ
by fulfilling the dreams of my father.

I look up to see the solemn figure,
who remains in perpetual vigil,
praying for peace.

I pray for Mary, Mother of all God's children.
I pray for Mary, mother of John, father to me.

May I be the true realization of the prayers
that young man made here years ago.

Did he ever imagine that I
would be the future he used to wonder about?

I can still feel his presence, like part of the rocks
that hold onto the prayers that
so many young people offer up to Her.

I pray for Dad, who loved this place.

ANONYMOUS

On the day of my marriage on August 22, 1970, in nearby Mishawaka, my wife and I paid a rather unusual visit to the Grotto. My brother, a member of the Congregation of Holy Cross, officiated at the wedding. In the late afternoon, after a brief reception, my bride and I agreed to drive my priest-brother back to Moreau Seminary on the Notre Dame campus. On the way to Notre Dame, I stopped at a relative's home and changed from my tuxedo into casual clothes. My bride, however, was still in her wedding gown. After dropping my brother at Moreau Seminary, we stopped at the Grotto to light a candle. I also wanted photos of my bride at the Grotto. It did not occur to us until some time later that the other visitors at the Grotto at the same time must have been mystified at the sight of a bride — but no groom!

CYRIL DE VLIEGHER
CLASS OF 1962
MISHAWAKA, INDIANA

I, like many others, consider the Grotto as my favorite spiritual respite. Something has always drawn me toward this solemn site; oftentimes it is the only place I visit when passing through the campus. Every Friday afternoon as a student I would spend a quiet moment kneeling before Our Lady, thanking Her for the many gifts that I had received during the week, and also asking for help and prayer for my family and loved ones. I particularly enjoyed staying on campus during the Thanksgiving and Easter breaks so that I could experience the peace and tranquility of the Grotto by myself (I never really considered this a selfish act). I inherited my special relationship with Mary from my mother and hope to pass this on to my children.

I do not have any stories of miracles or humorous occurrences, but the Grotto has provided me with the strength and understanding to make all of my important life decisions: medical school, residency training, employment, and marriage. In fact, the Grotto almost cost me my marriage. I delayed proposing to my wife for four months so that I could capture the beauty of the moment at the Grotto during a football weekend visit. She had almost ended the relationship, citing a lack of commitment. It must be an excellent location for proposing: my wife, mother and grandmother all said "yes." I doubt any woman could refuse a marriage proposal amidst the wonder of the Grotto.

I have often tried to put my many feelings toward the Grotto into words. This task is nearly impossible, but I think I can visualize the essence of the place. In fact, nearly every former Domer can picture the stillness and beauty of the Grotto with its candles flickering gently during a quiet evening's soft snowfall. I feel that this picture is truly worth a thousand feelings!

One of my memorable Notre Dame experiences relates to the Grotto in the Fall of 1987. At the time I was a graduate student, living in St. Joe Hall. A terrible tragedy had struck the Beauchamp family, just as Father Bill became the Executive Vice President. His parents, residing in Michigan, had been murdered. A twenty-four vigil was being conducted at the Grotto. It was one of those sultry September nights, and the hour had fallen in the still dark morning. I was just returning to my room at St. Joe and had earlier decided that I would go and spend some time at the vigil. As I approached the Grotto, passing my favorite campus tree, the willow, the warm glow of the full concert of flickering flames drew me in. The rich colors of the fall flowers blooming guided my walk. A sense of peace and of power overtook and enveloped me — sorrow yet union pervaded my spirit. With the exception of one other person, I was alone at the Grotto. I knelt in prayer, praying for Father Beauchamp's parents, for Bill and his whole family. This was the Notre Dame Community. This was Notre Dame.

JOHN BANGETTO
SCOTTS VALLEY, CALIFORNIA

At the beginning of October you could see the fall season in the green, yellow, brown and maroon leaves on the campus. The air smelled dry and burnt. The temperature was in the upper 50s during the day, which made sleeping in Howard Hall almost a joy since the steamy start we felt in September when we entered our second year in college. The time was October 1962 and everything was going well.

Dick, my roommate, and I settled into Howard for our sophomore year. We were close to the old Memorial Library, we had a few friends, and our confidence to succeed in college had markedly increased since last year. This cozy mood crumbled quickly when we saw television reports about missiles the Russians had covertly placed in Cuba. President Kennedy announced a tough political stance, calling for immediate and complete removal of the weapons. This was a clear case of a possible fight between the two most powerful countries in existence. We weren't watching two teenagers from Chicago argue about whose car was faster. Dick and I didn't talk a lot about the news reports but we knew that both of us were very worried. We talked regularly but there was little humor in our stories. Dick didn't say as much about his future wife, Kathy. I stopped wondering if and when I would get my own car. We had finished a fairly successful year at Notre Dame and thought we were over many of the obstacles found in the first year. We knew how to study for exams, where to hide to do serious work, when to line up for dinner in the South Dining Hall, and who to talk to for help. As we debated the moment in history that would become known as the "Cuban Missile Crisis," we were afraid to lose our comfortable circumstances and chances for success we dreamed about. Our families were not close to comfort us. I was a three hour drive from Chicago and Dick was at least a three hour flight from New Jersey. We were 19 years old and images of being drafted in the Army quickly came to mind. World War II ended when we learned to ride tricycles, and we began third grade during the Korean War. Was it now our time to face war?

We found it almost impossible to concentrate on classwork as everyone waited to see what would come of Kennedy's challenge to Khrushchev. How were we supposed to handle the anxiety from a confrontation that had such massive potential to destroy our way of life? This experience created feelings reminiscent of those from the A-bomb threats during the Cold War Fifties when bomb shelters were going to preserve our lives and when we practiced hiding under wooden desks to shield ourselves from nuclear attack.

In the past year Dick and I had gone to the Grotto to ask for insight and guidance with exams and term papers. We also liked walking around St. Mary's and St. Joseph's Lakes after dinner and always stopped to pray. We now sensed that going to the Grotto was the only action we could take to handle our feelings of disruption and possible loss. The evening was clear and comfortable as we approached from Howard. There weren't any more visitors than usual. We knelt on the hard metal frames, offered our petitions in silence and lit votive candles. I asked for peace and the chance to finish school. It was selfish to pray this way but we were frightened. I don't recall what we offered as our end of the bargain with Mary and her Son. We probably made it a one-sided request. After ten minutes of silent praying, lighting candles, and looking around, we walked away feeling relieved, as though a weight, a burden, a responsibility was lifted from us.

I don't remember how long it was before we heard that the Missile Crisis was over, but during the waiting period Dick and I did not worry as much as we had before our Grotto visit on that cool October evening in 1962.

MICHAEL P. BOCHENEK
CLASS OF 1965
HOFFMAN ESTATES, ILLINOIS

Everytime I return to campus for whatever reason, football games, reunions, or just for fun, I like to stop at the Grotto. The Grotto is a timeless place, somewhere between earth and heaven. One such time I was attending my husband's '76 reunion. Now most everyone has a great time at their own reunion, talking to classmates and catching up on the whereabouts of others. But, nothing can bring on boredom faster than being with a spouse as she/he engages in a lively conversation with classmates, and you are not from that class. On this particular occasion, as always, there were multiple reunions on campus. My dad had told me my uncle was attending his class reunion of '41. My husband and I searched for him in the dining hall but had not come across him. The noise coming from the beer tent on the north quad seemed to be getting louder as the night progressed. It was a warm night. I longed for some solitude. I slipped away, almost unnoticed, to the Grotto — my sanctuary. The rock and roll music was barely audible now. Who do you suppose I saw? Uncle Dick! If I had planned a time to see him it could not have worked out better. It was almost 11 p.m. Do you think Our Lady smiles down on her children who happen to meet there? Going back to the noisy beer tent was not so bad.

HOLLY (ZUEHLKE) BRANDWIE
CLASS OF 1981
VALPARAISO, INDIANA

My memories of Our Lady's Grotto at the University of Notre Dame span 50 years. I did not meet my husband until after he graduated from Notre Dame in 1943. He wanted us to be married in the Log Chapel on campus but that could not be at the time, 1945. However, the first stop on our honeymoon was the Grotto.

He told me that while he was in school, he visited the Grotto every day and prayed for a good wife and a large family, like his own with six siblings. We had 10 children and even though only one attended Notre Dame, they all visit the Grotto on football weekends. Now that my husband is gone and we are still fortunate to attend some games now and then, the first stop is the Grotto on Friday evening to light a candle for Dad and thank him for introducing us, so many years ago, to this beautiful, peaceful little spot.

JANE BOWLING (MRS. BERNARD F.)
LOUISVILLE, KENTUCKY

THE "SENIORS' LAST VISIT" to Sacred Heart and the Grotto is a tradition that evolved from the year-long celebration of the centennial of the Lourdes Grotto in 1958. The observance declined in the 1970s, and was revived in 1981 by Rev. John Fitzgerald, C.S.C., and Steven Warner of Campus Ministry. The seniors celebrate their Notre Dame experience in song, readings and poetry, with the Notre Dame Glee Club and Folk Choir.

Seniors' Last Visit
May 1995

My Grotto story is simple: Three times Our Lady has given me back my life.

I first came to Notre Dame and the Grotto in 1962 as a St. Mary's freshman. I looked, talked and acted like a typical upper middle class good Catholic girl from a large and happy family of nine children. At least that was how I presented myself. The interior confusion and anguish of having lived for many years in a chaotic family with two alcoholic parents (in a world where alcoholism didn't exist among "nice" people) was, I think, well hidden.

At Notre Dame I found peace and wonderful people who helped me find an inner core that I had lost in the turbulence of my birth home. Most importantly, I was gifted with a wonderful man who still loves me unconditionally after thirty+ years of marriage.

After graduation, my husband and I set about the business of living and raising a family. In 1985, we brought our oldest son to Notre Dame as an incoming freshman. The joy of that weekend was tempered by the knowledge that the family disease of alcoholism had taken hold of me. I wonder how many other parents sat through the Orientation weekend with a flask discreetly hidden on their persons. I suspect I was not the only one. The Saturday afternoon of Orientation weekend I left my family and took a long walk; back and forth along the path to St. Mary's, ending at the Grotto. I sat and meditated for a long time, remembering the girl I had been when I came to St. Mary's and facing the reality of the woman I had become. I asked Our Lady to help me do what I knew had to be done. Three weeks later I walked into my first AA meeting and I have been sober ever since.

Five years of sobriety brought much happiness and many wonderful changes to my life. In March of 1990 my husband and I came to Notre Dame for St. Patrick's Day. Our oldest son had graduated in 1989; his brother was a senior due to graduate in June. Gary was engaged to a lovely young woman (also a Domer) and the wedding would take place at Sacred Heart Basilica. Our youngest child, a daughter, had just been accepted as an incoming freshman for the ND Class of '94. That Friday, March 16, was an uncommonly beautiful and warm day. My husband suggested a walk around St. Joseph's Lake and we paused on the far side to look back at the campus landscape. I remember feeling a sense of perfect peace and happiness — so close to my husband and God and Our Lady. I have never felt like that before or since.

The next day turned cold and rainy. We stopped at the Grotto that night and as we were leaving I felt a slight nose bleed begin. Later that night I awoke with a massive hemorrhage from my nose. The final diagnosis was a rare form of cancer — a brain tumor that could only be removed by radical craniofacial surgery. I had the initial surgery and I was strangely unafraid. I could not forget that I had started to bleed at Our Lady's Grotto. I was not sure what that meant, but it was strangely reassuring.

January of 1991 found me still alive, but faced with a grave dilemma. The initial cancer surgery and subsequent infections had cost me my forehead bone plate. Doctors offered a chance at reconstructive surgery that could give me some semblance of normalcy — a cranioplasty that would take a piece of bone from the side of my head and be used to create a new forehead. There were no guarantees of a successful graft; potential complications from such surgery began with severe neurological impairment and grew worse. How to choose? By now I had learned that decisions such as these, too big and complex for ordinary people like me, belong to God. So I asked His Mother to please find out what I should do and let me know. As you see, the beauty of being very sick is that life becomes very simple.

On February 11 at noon, my phone rang. It was my doctor saying that, if I wanted to try the operation, it could be done on February 14. February 11 and 14 are the dates of the first two apparitions of Mary to Bernadette at the Lourdes Grotto. Some may call it coincidence or just plain silliness, but I will believe till I die that this was Mary's way of telling me her Son's answer — to go ahead and have the operation. It would be OK. I might mention that the operation was a complete success and I set new records for a quick recovery. I was up and walking about the day after surgery. I do not exaggerate when I say that the nurses and doctors on my floor could not believe what they were seeing. Of course it was hard to believe — it was a miracle in progress.

In 1996 I am still cancer-free and I am still in awe that Our Lady of the Grotto saw fit to intervene so directly in my life. I do not know where the journey will take us next, but I do know that I love to walk with her and, for some reason that I do not understand, I humbly feel that she likes to walk with me.

ANONYMOUS

It has been 33 years since a new Air Force Second Lieutenant left the relative shelter of the Notre Dame campus for the excitement of the fledgling space program at Cape Canaveral. The campus has seen many changes since then. New buildings have sprouted up, as some old ones disappeared; and females have joined the ranks of the student body! Upon returning to the campus; however, it is reassuring to know that one thing remains unchanged — the Grotto of Our Lady.

Reminiscing on my years at Notre Dame invoke many strong feelings. As a struggling freshman Aeronautical Engineering student, I knew these couldn't be, "the best years of my life," or at least I hoped they weren't! I remember an inscription over a portal, "For God, Country and Notre Dame." This inscription flooded my memory again during a few long dark nights lying in an Asian rice paddy. I also remember the weather; it was bad and the food was worse. My most calming remembrance of my brief stay at Notre Dame is the time I spent at the Grotto.

Morning Checks, as intended, made daily Mass and Communion a normal routine. In addition, I developed the habit of stopping by the Grotto to recite a quick decade and the Memorare. To the best of my memory, I visited the Grotto every day during my four years on campus. My visits occurred at all times of the day and night; in weather that included rain, sleet and snow (or all of the above).

The Grotto was like a short visit to the holodeck on the spaceship Enterprise. It was brief respite from the worries and pressures of student life. A time to thank Jesus and his Holy Mother for past assistance, and to ask for even more. Despite the weather or the next morning's exam, I always had a feeling of being refreshed as I trudged back to my residence hall and "night check."

While many of my associates considered my matriculation a miracle, I doubt it would pass the rigors of close examination by a Papal commission. Of one fact I'm sure, there was considerable divine assistance provided on my route to the eventual award of a sheepskin.

Some would say the late '50s and early '60s were a gentler time and that today's students have different agendas, but I'm not sure that assessment is correct. Notre Dame students today probably deal with the same pressures we faced many years ago; tight class schedules, deadlines, insurmountable amounts of homework and the ever present exams. Most likely, Notre Dame students of today are not much different than we were 30+ years ago, except today they may be dating their classmates — a practice which was definitely frowned upon during my tenure.

My time kneeling at the Grotto is my strongest remembrance of Notre Dame and one I will carry with me until it's time for the ultimate journey.

GREG RISCH
CLASS OF 1962
NICEVILLE, FLORIDA

When I first came to Notre Dame in 1959, the lights were turned off in the dorms every evening at 11 o'clock. So the Grotto soon became a source for candles to use when periodically, after a quick Hail Mary, I would approach the cave's interior beneath Mary's mantle — in a "prayerful" posture, of course — and cop a couple of candles to help cope with a week's work. God forgive me if I did not slip some change into the coin box. Even after the lights were lit permanently my junior year, I tried to include a path to the Grotto, without the wax merchandise, as part of my daily destinations. And a return to the campus today is not complete unless it includes a visit to the Lourdes Lady near the lakes. I've read inspirational words about the Grotto and photographed the place in all seasons, day and night. But there's nothing like being there amidst the quiet beauty of Mary's presence within those tree-lined rocks. One can't help but gaze on the blackened boulders above the flickering flames and wonder about the plethora of prayers murmured by many for nearly a century.

One visit during the winter of 1994 I'll never forget. While staying at the Morris Inn, a sudden snow storm struck South Bend. I was reminded of Tom Dooley's words about how he missed seeing the Grotto in snow. So I dutifully set out for the hallowed haven to see the winter wonder for myself and join in the daily recitation of the Rosary at 7 p.m. The snow seemed to awaken the sleepy shadows surrounding the shrine. The candles' glow completely cut off the night that had earlier engulfed the entire campus. Standing alone in the snow for several minutes, I wondered if the Rosary responsibility would remain only mine. Suddenly, four figures emerged from the far side of Sacred Heart Basilica and descended the stairs to the Grotto and took cover beneath the rock-constructed canopy. As a visitor to their established Rosary routine, I decided to remain outside the shelter of the shrine. Besides, by now, the snow had nearly completely covered me and I felt a sort of sacredness in remaining stationery. I don't think I've ever experienced a more moving or reverent Rosary. It seemed a perfect prayer as part of the snow. I marvelled at the motivation of the men, at least one a priest, who braved a blizzard to pray. And I half congratulated myself for also stepping out into the storm, perhaps to see if there would be any Ave's at all on such an awful night.

VINCE LABARBERA
CLASS OF 1963
FORT WAYNE, INDIANA

BROTHER JOHN LAVELLE began
the nightly Rosary recitation,
sometime before 1981.

Dr. Thomas A. Dooley, III, Class of 1948, won worldwide recognition when he brought medical relief to Southeast Asians during the 1950s. He was presented with numerous humanitarian awards, including the Congressional Medal of Honor, the Legion of Merit Award and the National Award of Vietnam, the country's highest honor bestowed upon a foreigner. He was the recipient of the first World Humanitarian Award. Dooley inspired President John F. Kennedy to establish the Peace Corps.

Six weeks before his death, Dooley wrote to Rev. Theodore Hesburgh, C.S.C., then-president of Notre Dame. His letter is mounted at the Grotto.

Hong Kong, December 2, 1960

Dear Father Hesburgh,

They've got me down. Flat on my back ... with plaster, sand bags and hot water bottles. It took the last three instruments to do it however. I've contrived a way of pumping the bed up a bit so that, with a long reach, I can get to my typewriter ... my mind ... my brain ... my fingers.

Two things prompt this note to you, sir. The first is that whenever my cancer acts up ... and it is certainly "acting up" now, I turn inward a bit. Less do I think of my hospitals around the world, or of 94 doctors, fund raising and the like. More do I think of one divine Doctor, and my own personal fund of grace. Is it enough?

It has become pretty definite that the cancer has spread to the lumbar vertebrae, accounting for all the back problems over the last two months. I have monstrous phantoms ... as all men do. But I try to exorcise them with all the fury of the middle ages. And inside and outside the wind blows.

But when the time comes, like now, then the storm around me does not matter. The winds within me do not matter. Nothing human or earthly can touch me. A wilder storm of peace gathers in my heart. What seems unpossessable, I can possess. What seems unfathomable, I fathom. What is unutterable, I utter. Because I can pray. I can communicate. How do people endure anything on earth if they cannot have God?

I realize the external symbols that surround one when he prays are not important. The stark wooden cross on an altar of boxes in Haiphong with a tortured priest ... the magnificence of the Sacred Heart Bernini altar ... they are essentially the same. Both are symbols. It is the Something Else there that counts.

But just now ... and just so many times, how I long for the Grotto. Away from the Grotto, Dooley just prays. But at the Grotto, especially now when there must be snow everywhere and the lake is ice glass and that triangular fountain on the left is frozen solid and all the priests are bundled in their too-large, too-long old black coats and the students wear snow boots ... if I could go to the Grotto now, then I think I could sing inside. I could be full of faith and poetry and loveliness and know more beauty, tenderness, and compassion. This is soggy sentimentalism, I know, (old prayers from a hospital bed are just as pleasing to God as more youthful prayers from a Grotto on the lid of night).

But like telling a mother in labor, "It's okay, millions have endured the labor pains and survived happy ... you will, too." It's consoling ... but doesn't lessen the pain. Accordingly, knowing prayers from here are just as good as from the Grotto doesn't lessen my gnawing, yearning passion to be there.

I don't mean to ramble. Yes, I do.

The second reason I write to you just now is that I have in front of me the *Notre Dame Alumnus* of September 1960. And herein is a story. This is a Chinese hospital run by a Chinese division of the Sisters of

Charity. (I think) Though my doctors are British, the hospital is as Chinese as Shark's Fin Soup. Every orderly, corpsman, nurse and nun know of my work in Asia, and each has taken it upon themselves to personally "give" to the man they feel has given to their Asia. As a consequence I'm a bit smothered in tender, loving care.

With a triumphant smile this morning one of the nuns brought me some American magazines (which are limp with age and which I must hold horizontal above my head to read ...) An old National Geographic, two older Times, and that unfortunate edition of Life ... and with these, a copy of the *Notre Dame Alumnus*. How did it ever get here?

So Father Hesburgh, Notre Dame is twice on my mind ... and always in my heart. That Grotto is the rock to which my life is anchored. Do the students ever appreciate what they have, while they have it? I know I never did. Spent most of my time being angry at the clergy at school ... 10 p.m. bed check, absurd for a 19-year-old veteran, etc., etc., etc.

Won't take any more of your time, did just want to communicate for a moment, and again offer my thanks to my beloved Notre Dame. Though I lack a certain buoyancy in my bones just now, I lack none in my spirit. I must return to the states very soon, and I hope to sneak into that Grotto ... before the snow has melted.

My best wishes to the students, regards to the faculty, and respects to you.

Very sincerely,

Tom Dooley

Dooley also spoke of the Grotto in a letter written to a classmate on May 25, 1959, from the Village of Muong Sing: "Oh, to be able to get on my knees in the Grotto of Our Lady just now! I know that God is everywhere. He's everywhere here. We see Him daily in 100 wretched who come to the clinic. We see Him in the mountains. We see Him in the monsoon rainfall on the thatched roof. We know Him when He outstretches His arm in the thunder. But to be in the Grotto at Notre Dame; there I find propinquity. There I have nearness that no rationalization can replace."

FROM THE THOMAS DOOLEY COLLECTION
UNIVERSITY ARCHIVES

ON OCTOBER 15, 1985, a statue of Tom Dooley with two Laotian children was placed along the path just west of the Grotto. The plaque on the statue reads: "Thomas A. Dooley, M.D. '48, 1927-1961. Who as a pre-med student cherished Our Lady's Grotto and who as a physician served the afflicted people of Southeast Asia with uncommon devotion and dedication.

Gift of the Notre Dame Club of St. Louis and the sculptor, Rudolph E. Torrini '59

Three years after Dooley's death, Father Thomas O'Donnell wrote about his now-famous letter to Father Hesburgh: "Sickness is a great thought provoker. When a person knows his disease or affliction is terminal he reaches back and grasps the great moments that helped him in the past and perhaps can help him now. This was the way with Tom Dooley. With aching fingers, he spoke his heart on a typewriter. It does the soul good and warms our hearts to pause in our haste and remember the unhastening hours and the sun that dials its seasons on the aging stone of the Grotto."

FROM *Notre Dame Alumnus*
FEBRUARY/MARCH, 1964

The only thing I can recall about my first visit to the Grotto was my surprise at finding the words of Tom Dooley there. I had read about him in high school but I was not aware of his connection to Notre Dame. A bond was immediately established.

My regular visits to the Grotto began in sophomore year when a shortcut between the dorm and one of my classes took me by that tranquil place. I remember feeling slightly drawn to it. Sometimes I would stop for just a moment — as if to say hello — and then move on. At other times I would say a brief prayer before an exam or wish that a letter from a girlfriend back home would arrive that day. And some days I just went there to sit and think. It was so soothing.

Life at Notre Dame had been okay but the whole experience had not been totally satisfying. Adjusting had been difficult. I was becoming more and more uneasy. I didn't understand it at the time, but now I know what was happening: By sophomore year, my childhood was catching up with me. Growing up with an abusive, alcoholic mother and a sometimes violent father was beginning to haunt me. Anxiety and depression became daily companions. I had difficulty concentrating and my grades began to fall. My friends thought I had become temperamental and antisocial. The smart thing to do would have been to go for help, but nineteen year olds don't always do the smart thing. I was too ashamed to talk about it.

I turned to the Grotto more and more. It gradually became the only place I could find any peace. I began to worry about the younger siblings I had left at home, still trapped in the web of the alcoholic family. They didn't have the luxury of being able to get away from the madness for months at a time, as I did.

In my junior year the relationship with the girlfriend back home ended and I was all alone in my torment. Shortly thereafter, insomnia set in. During the day, one rarely had the Grotto to oneself. But at 3 a.m. it was mine alone. The quiet was broken only by the wind blowing across the lake or the rustling of leaves. I prayed for my siblings, for peace at home and for strength to go on. I steadied myself and made it to graduation.

My years at Notre Dame were not happy ones. But when I go back there now for a reunion or a football game I have a warm feeling all over. I no longer lament a childhood lost nor a college experience missed, but I am extremely grateful that such a place exists. For Notre Dame and her Grotto held me and comforted me when I needed it most.

Yes, Tom Dooley, some of us did appreciate what we had when we had it.

ANONYMOUS

1996 marks the 100th anniversary of the Lourdes Grotto at Notre Dame and the 46th year of my involvement on the University of Notre Dame campus. During that time, the Grotto has meant more to me than any other campus landmark: more inspiration, more spiritual charge and, in times of despair, more consolation. I first set eyes on the Grotto when, quite by accident, on my first day on campus in 1950, I found myself sitting there in despair and confusion, after having been told by the good Brother Superior that, in his opinion, I really didn't want to be a Holy Cross Brother. It was here, to the Grotto, that I brought my troubled mind and it was here, by the grace of God, that an unidentified Brother appeared who, recognizing my torment, suggested that perhaps I would be more interested in training to be a Brother in the Priests' Province. These Brothers, be said, were trained to work in offices and departments at Notre Dame, an exciting and rewarding life about which Father Daniel O'Neill, the vocations director, would be happy to talk with me. Even in the short time I had been on campus, I sensed that this was a special place where one could find happiness in a dedicated life. I agreed to talk with Father O'Neill and set in motion the wheels that would take me on a long journey, fascinating and exciting, through the worlds of spirituality and sports on the Notre Dame campus. Though this journey has culminated in a full circle, taking me back to the Grotto where it began, the journey is not over. In these, my "retirement" years, I seldom miss a Rosary at the Grotto, often leading the hymn singing and praying of the decades. Sometimes on a cold and blustery Christmas Eve, when the students have abandoned the campus and snow covers the ground around the Nativity scene, Brother Beatus and I are the only semblance of the faithful, but the Rosary is recited. And usually, at some point during these Christmas Eve rosaries, Brother Dennis, chief sacristan of Sacred Heart Basilica, can be seen trudging through the snow to place the infant Jesus in the crib.

Senior years are an adventure, I believe, a special gift from God. I count my days in privileged moments, the most rewarding of these moments coming at the end of each day in prayer at the Grotto. It is a constant reminder of the peaceful beauty of God's creation, leading me beyond what can be seen to the Unseen One who walks beside me on life's journey. Perhaps I am most indebted to the Grotto because it was there that I received the inspiration for the ministries which have kept me active in the Lord's work. The first fruits of this inspiration was SERV, Students Encouraging Religious Vocations, approved by the University in 1990 and still showing tangible evidence of success. On the heels of this success came the inspiration for The National Legion of SERV, helping high schools, colleges and parish vocation committees around the country to establish SERV clubs. Most recently came the inspiration for the Saint Peregrine Prayer Society, an international network of people praying to Saint Peregrine for his intercession to bring down God's healing and compassion on those who suffer from cancer and other life-threatening diseases.

Unlike the Golden Dome, Notre Dame's familiar landmark and shining symbol of its tradition, the Grotto touches lives in a quiet, more meaningful and precious way. If I were to pick the perfect time and place to extol the beauty, both natural and spiritual, of the Notre Dame campus, it most certainly would be 6:45 in the evening at the Grotto. It is precisely at that moment, every day of the year, without exception, that the Holy Rosary is recited in devotion to the Lady after whom the University is named. And it is at that time, for the better part of the year, that the sun is setting beyond the mirrored lake of St. Mary's, splashing its rays of reds, pinks and blues across the stone face of the Grotto and onto the white and blue image of Our Lady as she looks down from her perch in the rocks.

I have already mentioned the Grotto's warmth on a blustery winter's eve. The days of summer, too, are a time of grace at the Grotto. The quiet evenings when we are joined by a few summer school students trying in six short weeks to become a part of the spirit of the place. And autumn, of course, is that special time of year when Mother Nature spreads her most colorful carpet; when red fires smolder on trees, on ivy-covered walls, and on the eternal stone face of the Grotto, drawing to itself the multitudes of football fans who descend on the campus. I cannot count the number of people I have met at the Grotto who have become life-long friends and partners in prayer. I would be willing to forfeit the rest of my life if I could be buried in the immediate vicinity of my beloved Grotto. That being impossible, however, it fills my heart with peace knowing that I will be buried in the Notre Dame addition to Cedar Grove Cemetery, just a short walk from the Grotto's peaceful and serene surroundings.

How many lives have been touched by this monument to Mary? How many tears have been shed in relief at her feet? Like the mysteries of the Rosary itself, they embrace the joyful, the sorrowful and the glorious.

> VISIBLE SIGNS of lives touched are the three "Favor Granted" plaques on the rock of the Grotto. Plaques are no longer allowed. The earliest plaque reads: "February 26, 1918. G.F and A.M." A second dated January 28, 1951, bears the initials, J.L.B. and the last: August 3, 1954 with initials M.H.M. A diamond-shaped recess on the left side of the Grotto is all that remains of a plaque that read "In remembrance of the First Pilgrimage from Holy Trinity Parish, Chicago, IL June 30, 1907," followed by the same message in Polish. It disappeared in the early 1920's.

HERB JULIANO
NOTRE DAME, INDIANA

I had about as much business going to Notre Dame as my old Pastor had in judging beauty contests. My world was an Italian neighborhood from which I wandered very infrequently. My world was pasta on Sunday, soup on Monday. But I wanted to go to Notre Dame, and I did. I wanted to cheer for the Fighting Irish, and I did. How I made it to Notre Dame is a mystery. How I survived is not.

I was a piece of buttered Italian bread waiting to be dipped in a cup of coffee. There was so much to learn and absorb at Notre Dame, things I was unaware of in 1947, fresh out of South Philadelphia: Like saying "good morning" to neighbors instead of looking at my shoelaces. Or holding a door open for someone behind me as I went in or out of a building — and the world of academics (a wonderland.) So there I was going from my constricted city block mentality to a place populated by the world — and the Grotto.

The Grotto became a daily stop for me — no problem. I needed Her more that She needed me. After supper at the dining hall, straight to the Grotto, also no problem, except on Sunday. And who was the culprit that caused me to stray, or think about straying? Jack Benny. His radio broadcast on Sunday evenings somehow always coincided with my departure from the dining hall. I couldn't break the cycle. It was soul searching and gut wrenching, but out of deference to Her age and powerful friends, the Lady won (most of the times.) I hope the two of them are enjoying this outpouring of guilt and baring of my soul.

FRANK MICHAEL TRIPODI
CLASS OF 1951
PHILADELPHIA, PENNSYLVANIA

In the fall of 1981, when I had been at Notre Dame only a couple of weeks, I was feeling a little homesick so I went to the Grotto for a few quiet moments. My father, a Notre Dame grad, told me it was the best place to be when you need a friend. When I arrived there I noticed a man praying alone and I stood silently next to him for a few moments until he turned to leave. It was then I recognized him — Gerry Faust. It was the night before the first home game of his first season at Notre Dame. I suppose he was feeling homesick, too. I wished him luck in the game and he thanked me and left. He didn't have the best record, but we did win the LSU game the next day and I knew someone was helping him!

CHERYL COOK
CLASS OF 1985
HAMDEN, CONNECTICUT

My mother died when I was a senior in high school and one of her wishes for growing older was to see me graduate college. Being the youngest of eight I figured she would always be around and I would tell her that she would see me married with kids. Sadly, none of that came to pass, at least not physically. I know my mother was with me at my high school graduation and I feel her with me and my family today. I also know she was watching over me the day I graduated from Notre Dame by a sign I received at the Grotto.

On my way to the graduation ceremony at the Joyce Center I stopped by the Grotto to say a prayer of thanks and to light a candle for my mother. There I was, clad in my cap and gown on a sunny, hot and humid May 16. As I knelt and said my prayers the thunder clouds began to roll in and just as I began to light the candle the skies opened up and the rain came pouring down. Five minutes I watched the rain fall and prayed to my mother thanking her for all that she had done and wishing that she was there, all the while I was safe and dry in that haven we call the Grotto. Some would say it was luck, a meteorologist would say it was natural, but that rain stopped just in time for me to make it to graduation and there were a lot of wet graduates who weren't so luck to be in such a safe and dry place.

Notre Dame, Our Lady, and my lady, my mom, have even come to me in a daily reminder on my license plate. When Pennsylvania started producing the Notre Dame alumni license plates I ordered one thinking it was pretty unusual for a private out-of-state school to get enough support to warrant their own alumni plate. The only drawback was that you had to take whatever number you got based on the sequence of the order. Well, either luck or the intervention of the two ladies up above sent me a sign of their love and support by making my plate number my mother's birthdate. No visit to campus is complete without a visit to the Grotto. I visited it often as an undergrad, but since it has been five years since my last visit, I wish I had stopped by more.

BRIAN J. FOGARTY
CLASS OF 1988
BALA-CYNWYD, PENNSYLVANIA

While visiting my son at Notre Dame, we were involved in a spirited conversation over one of his impending essays and about 1:45 a.m. I said: "Chris, I've got to get some sleep — let's turn in." "Dad," he replied, "Would you mind going somewhere with me first?" Astonished I said, "Where in the world do you want to go at this time of night?"

"I always like to pay a visit to the grotto before I go to bed," he answered. Gladly I accompanied him and as we approached the grotto about 2 a.m., I could see twelve other young men and women kneeling there. Gratefully, we joined them and as we later turned to leave, my son said, "You know, dad, it sounds silly, but every once in a while, I think I see her hand move towards me."

What a blessed memory he created for his father that night!

CHUCK PERRIN
CLASS OF 1950, 1951 J.D.
VENICE, FLORIDA

Words are inadequate when one feels deeply. Such is the case here.

Our eleven-month-old grandson was brought to us for a visit — a visit which turned into a ten year stay. Sixty-six and sixty-one, respectively, when circumstances made it evident we would be pivotal in his rearing, we were apprehensive and overwhelmed. A visit to the Grotto — a still, small voice eased all that. My lament about not having the stamina to do my work and care for a baby at this point in my life was put to rest. "This is the most important work in your life" my senses dictated. Acceptance has been the key, though some days were pretty rough.

With an assist from Barney, his Guardian Angel, prayers to and for his Daddy, now deceased, our daughter (his Mom) who was left to care for him as a single parent and prays to everyone up there who takes the time to listen, Daniel Francis Ford is growing up to be a fine young man. They are now in their own home due to our daughter's prowess and hard work, and, of course, much, much prayer.

MRS. RALPH PRZESTWOR
SOUTH BEND, INDIANA

When I was a bride of one month, in the fall of 1967, my husband (Philip J. Rauen, Class of 1958) took me to my first Notre Dame football game. Having had a lifelong devotion to the Blessed Virgin Mary, I was enthralled with the Grotto; the devotion of others that I saw there. I prayed that I would someday have a son, and that he could someday attend Notre Dame.

One year later, we had our son — but my husband had his first attack of Multiple Sclerosis, at age 30. On our next trip to Notre Dame and the Grotto, I prayed that my husband would not only stay sufficiently well to work, but that he would be successful enough to afford Notre Dame when our son grew up.

My son, Phillip J. Rauen IV, did graduate from Notre Dame, even though my husband became completely disabled in my son's junior year. Because most people afflicted with MS are unable to work 22 years; because our son was brilliant enough to get into Notre Dame; and because we were able to afford his education, we know that my prayers as a bride and as a mother, were indeed answered by the Blessed Virgin at the Grotto.

For Junior Parents' Weekend at Notre Dame, my son gave me a corsage for the final dinner. (I did not know that this was the custom and I was pleased for many reasons.) Not wanting to bring the corsage back to Kansas, I thought I would take it to the Grotto to place at the foot of Mary's statue. Thinking my idea was original, I was quite surprised to find hundreds of mothers had the same idea — and all the corsages and centerpieces were there. As I knelt there praying and feeling very foolish for having thought I was the only one with this idea, I looked up to see Father Hesburgh standing in front of all the flowers, praying. And he raised his hand and blessed all of the flowers. I am certain that it was Mary's way of telling her devotee that this sincere offering of my son's flowers to me were pleasing to her and her son.

EVELYN L. RAUEN
OVERLAND PARK, KANSAS

The rainbow photograph on the back cover of Grotto Stories *was taken by Richard L. Spicer of South Bend.*
During the 1960s he delivered newspapers on campus. He always admired the Grotto on his daily delivery to Columbo Hall.
He captured the rainbow in the first photograph he took with his new camera early one February morning in 1981.
He was not aware of the effect until the film was developed. Mr. Spicer made the observation that the dove-shaped patch of snow
on the left side of the Grotto seems to be flying toward the Virgin Mary who appears to be standing on a cloud.

John J. Gaido, Jr. wrote the following tribute to the Grotto, titled "Thoughts on a Sunday Afternoon," in 1954, as a sophomore at Notre Dame. The essay was discovered by his daughter, Mary Kathryn Gaido Werner in 1995, two years after his death.

Upon the University of Notre Dame campus there is a shrine dedicated to our Lady of Lourdes. It has been constructed to resemble the now famous shrine at Lourdes, France. Here, a facsimile of the original Grotto commemorates the appearance of the Blessed Mother to the peasant girl, Bernadette. The Grotto at Notre Dame is not internationally known. It has never shared even a fraction of the publicity afforded to this University's football team. But, to the students, to the alumni, to the priests and sisters of the Holy Cross, to many of the visitors to this campus, and to friends of Notre Dame, it has a quiet fame and is a place of high importance in their hearts. For the people who know the Grotto well, it is the first place to visit when they come to campus and the last place to visit when they leave.

If one would take some time to observe the Grotto, it would seem that there is always somebody there. A student in his sweatshirt, a priest in his black robe, a young couple, an old man, an important visitor, a curious tourist ... Why the attraction? Why the attention? To those of us who have visited the Grotto many times, these questions are easy to answer. But it is hard to explain certain things in words that must be felt by the heart and accepted by one's faith.

Somehow, there a cold day does not seem so cold; a hot day, not so hot; and a rainy day, not as damp as other places on the campus. The pleasant sunny days are even more beautiful at the Grotto. The Grotto itself is a shallow cave, built with common Indiana granite rocks and reinforced with cement. Its back is against a small hill, which is behind Sacred Heart Church on the campus. Above, behind, around, and in front of the shrine, tall pines, stately oaks and maples, and leafy shrubbery lend their green beauty to the scene. While standing before the Grotto, one can see the brilliant gold of the dome of the Administration Building glistening in the sun. An iron railing and kneeler encloses the entrance to the cave, and within the cave itself are several candle stands. The walls of the cave are blackened with the carbon of the continually burning candles. To the right, and slightly above the larger cave, in a small nook or crevice, rests the statue of the Blessed Virgin Mary as she appeared to Bernadette. She is dressed in white, holding a rosary, golden roses at her feet, and a halo with the words, "Oh, Mary, Conceived Without Sin, Pray For Us," surrounds her. Before her, on the ground, kneels a small whitewashed statue of Bernadette. A park-like area stretches in front of the shrine, with green grass and benches, to the shores of St. Mary's Lake. Still and placid, its surface rippled only by a slight breeze, and its clear color contrasted by the billowy white of a few swimming swans.

At the Grotto, the air is clean and fresh. The wind stirs the trees just enough to provide a soft orchestral background to the choirs of birds that inhabit the area. During the day, the Grotto is bright with reflected light from the lake, but shaded from the direct rays of the sun by the many trees. At night, the atmosphere becomes more solemn. The scene is lit only by the burning devotional candles. Deep and somber shadows take the place of vivid details, and a new beauty is presented in the light of the flickering candles. The statue of Mary is always visible. She seems to smile down at this scene of tranquility, which is especially appropriate for the Queen of Heaven. There is offered the peace, hope, help, and understanding that only a Heavenly Mother can provide.

Could not a miracle be a relative thing? Is this day of reason, science, and society so far advanced that it is no longer fashionable that God helps us if we pray to His Mother and ask for help. To be a miracle, does the happening have to be publicized and acclaimed by the Church? Could there not be little personal miracles, important, oh so very important, to those to whom they happened?

In May, the month dedicated to the Blessed Virgin Mary, the night shadows of the Grotto are dispelled by five thousand pinpoints of light, as the students of the University pay homage to the Mother of God. The termination of a procession, which winds its way across the campus, is Her shrine. From every dormitory, the students come, a candle carried by each one, a rosary in their hands. The Rosary is completed enroute, and Benediction of the Blessed Sacrament is offered on the small altar at the right of the Grotto. A few words are said about the Virgin, and hymns of praise are offered to her. Those who take part in this simple ceremony leave with a clean peaceful feeling. There is the birth of new hope and new nourishment for the soul and the mind.

Once on the night of this May procession, the air was hot and sultry, the night sky split and illuminated with ragged streaks of lightening. The prayers of the students were drowned out by the rumbling of heavy thunder, and the whistling fury of the wind. The rest of the campus received a drenching downpour. There was no rain at the Grotto and the candles of faith remained burning. There are many scientific explanations possible for this phenomena, but those there at the time were sure that the Blessed Mother smiled down at her sons that night in their efforts to please her.

Many people come to the Grotto. Their reasons and their prayers are greatly diversified. For many months an older couple brought their son to the Grotto. The three of them would sit there for an hour or so, on one of the benches. The man and woman looked at Mary. The son, crippled and deformed, was unable to focus his eyes. Not a word did they utter, but each day would sit in silent vigil. One day, the son was not with them, and never was he seen again. But daily, they returned. Perhaps now they prayed to the Heavenly Mother to care for their child and somehow they knew he would never suffer again in her loving care.

Many different requests, thanksgivings, and sorrowful stories must have been heard by Mary at the Grotto. A plea to win a game, a request for a passing mark, a petition to find the right girl for a wife and mother of a good Catholic family, a prayer for peace, and so many others have had their turn here. And then there are the thanksgivings for a wonderful vacation, a passing exam, a football victory, and for being alive in a world blessed by a loving God. So very many have experienced a feeling of pride, of special honor, and of such sweet love, when they brought that special person to Mary and presented her to his Heavenly Mother.

Formal prayers, deep meditation, and long sermons would not be out of place here. But, it seems more natural to feel that this is a favorite spot of Mary, who is the Mother of us all. Therefore, I don't think she minds at all when one of her visitors just says, "Hello, Mary." And stops to talk to her. It seems so easy to talk to her as a mother there.

It will remain forever, a hallowed spot on the University of Notre Dame campus. It will be remembered by those who have been there, and the countless number to follow, as the Grotto continues to bring hope, help, and understanding into a troubled world.

JOHN JOSEPH GAIDO, JR.
CLASS OF 1956

As I reside in Columba Hall, a long and hefty stone's throw from the Grotto, I rather feel as a self-appointed "custodian," Guardian of Our Lady's cave there. I often sit on the bench dedicated to my classmate, (and my predecessor as Class Secretary, 1934) Ed Moran. The Grotto is a sacred place and silence belongs to the sacred. My observations are that in the midst of this savored silence, down the steps rushes a tidal wave of chattering youngsters, shattering the quiet. A custodian's signal from below, a mere raising a finger to the lips, would silence them.

I might be seen entering, placing money for a candle but walking away without igniting one. I am actually paying back debts, without interest, for candles filched during my student days for late-night cramming before exams, as all lights on campus went out at 11 p.m. I never felt like a thief as scads of other scholars were doing likewise. All of us, I am sure, intended to eventually pay back.

It's Wednesday, June 21, 1995. I witness a column of up to 700 summer camp kids troop by, ages circa 12 to 16, all male, topped with the sacred baseball caps. They are headed for the Grotto. Now, to see how they behave down there. Following close behind, I stand amazed. Their several adult leaders have alerted them, requesting silence and removal of their beloved headpieces. After five minutes they departed talking in reverent low voices. Unbelievable! Then I am brought back down to earth: Down the steps comes another wave of same aged boys with adult leaders, all chattering, the leaders bellowing orders. The chatter continues and the caps stay on. Kids are rushing for the benches, pushing and shoving. At that moment I appointed myself custodian. I turn to the boys nearest me who are cackling away and say: "Silence, please. This is a shrine, not a play-ground." They are silent. While the group is still there churning around, down the right steps comes a tour of about 30 ladies. Not to become further involved, I tiptoe away as my eye catches sight of another campus tour approaching from behind Corby Hall. But who knows what inspiration took place among those up to 1,000 souls during that half-hour. After all, Our Lady is in charge of her Grotto!

VINCE FERRER MCALOON, SPQR
CLASS OF 1934
NOTRE DAME, INDIANA

I had a friend named Lucy Pilkinton. Lucy was also my neighbor for ten years. We shared a common outlook on life and a love for the Grotto of Our Lady of Lourdes at Notre Dame. But the only time that we visited the Grotto together was late evening on January 31, 1993, the night before my surgery for cancer. My prognosis was poor and I was filled with worry, fearing that I would not live to raise my children. Lucy, however, exuded optimism. The trip to the Grotto was both her invitation and her expression of a faith that could conquer the bad news of doctors. Lucy drove us there and spoke reassuringly. The night was cold with some snow on the ground but also clear with a poignant stillness. We parked near the Grotto because Lucy was a Notre Dame employee and had a special sticker on her car window.

We knelt at the Grotto railing and gazed at the statue face of Our Lady. I prayed my desperate request for prolonged life. Then, we arose and lit candles. My special intention was for a complete recovery, a total healing. Lucy lit a candle for my family for she was aware of their mental suffering and their need for solace. We left in peace.

The following January, 1994, Lucy died suddenly of a brain aneurysm that burst while she was teaching a class at Notre Dame. She was in good health and good cheer at the time. She did not know that she had a brain aneurysm. I mourned her death as I have never mourned the death of another human being. It has been over two years since I had the surgery for cancer and my doctors, while cautious, are also expressing optimism. Lucy's faith was contagious. Through her faith and gift of friendship, I do indeed feel renewed in life. There are times when it seems to me that I even sense her presence. That this should be so does not surprise me. After all, Jesus conquered death. The Mary who appeared to Bernadette at Lourdes was very much alive. The Lourdes Grotto at Notre Dame will forever be a reminder to me of the soul's survival because my evening visit there with Lucy made it so.

ANNE RAYMER
SOUTH BEND, INDIANA

A PRE-FIRE PHOTO of the Grotto thick with ivy.

It was the summer of 1993 when I first took my daughter, Sara, to visit Notre Dame. Living, as we did then, in South Florida, it was an opportunity I had looked forward to for quite some time: To instill in her a love for Our Lady's campus. Sara was all of three and a half years old, tow-headed blonde, blue eyes, chipper and cheerful. More than any parent could ask or hope for.

Summer days at Notre Dame, as I knew from years past, were warm, serene, and filled with a transcendent peace, peopled with religious professed and otherwise. I urged respectful quiet as we visited Sacred Heart Basilica, departed from the west transept and journeyed toward the Grotto. Aware that the evening Rosary was being prayed, I again reminded Sara to be quiet. All was well until we started to descend the steps, when my sweet child, overcome with wonder, burst outloud, "Mommy, it's so beautiful!" Heads at the Rosary turned toward the interruption, then burst out loud in delighted laughter upon seeing the source of their distraction. Welcomed by bemused eyes, we sat through the remainder of the Rosary. Afterward, as we made our way to light some candles, not a few people stopped us to express their desire to take Sara home with them, or to inquire if perhaps there were another like her at the bookstore ...

As a student at Notre Dame, my prayers at the Grotto often arose out of a sense of searching and confusion, clueless as to my future, my major, my raison d'etre. Prayers like that are seldom answered instantly, as if a fax or e-mail from above were possible. Or as my now five-and-a-half-year-old says: "Somebody tell God to talk louder because I can't hear Him!" But I know, as clear as a child's laughter, that my Grotto prayers have been answered. And I look forward to the time when my answer and I can again return, in thanks, in praise and wonder, and to perhaps sow a few more seeds. Not for my future, but for hers.

PATRICIA METCALF KLEPPER
CLASS OF 1977
WENTZVILLE, MISSOURI

"Out of our reflection at the Grotto comes an understanding of Mary as a woman closer to God than any of us will ever be ...
She adds her own special sweetness to our prayers — which must make them endearing to Him.
I love the Grotto. It's free of pretentiousness, like the child Bernadette whom the Mother of God chose to visit ...
The Grotto that I'm homesick for when I'm away, is a summer place ..."

Rev. Robert Griffin, "Going Home to God By Way of the Grotto,"
The Observer, *May 1992*

Once upon a time, a girl was admitted to the University of Notre Dame, but alas, her boyfriend was denied entry. The girl visited Notre Dame to please her parents, but her heart wasn't in the visit. She went to the Grotto. She wouldn't light a candle. She didn't pray to the Virgin Mary or to Jesus or to God, she railed against them. How could they do this to someone she loved? It wasn't fair. Didn't they care that they had broken his heart? How could they be so cruel and hurtful? She would show them. She wouldn't go to Notre Dame either.

The next spring, the boy decided to apply to Notre Dame again. The girl was worried that his heart would be broken once more. The letter came. He had been admitted! The girl visited him for a football weekend. She went to the Grotto. She lit a candle. She thanked the Virgin Mary and Jesus and God for admitting her boyfriend to the school. She thanked them for teaching her patience and humility.

Prayers are funny things. They do get answered. This couple is now happily married.

ANONYMOUS

I used to pray the Rosary at the local abortion clinic in South Bend with a group of students every Friday afternoon. Once, when I missed the ride to the clinic, I decided to go to the Grotto to pray. I knelt down to pray the Rosary before the Statue of Our Lady, but forgot what mysteries to pray about. (I had always prayed the Rosary in a group which led the prayers). I apologized sincerely, promised I would learn the mysteries and quickly left. As I walked back to Walsh Hall, something caught my eye. Under the leaves on the sidewalk in front of Sorin Hall was a blue pamphlet with the mysteries of the Rosary and a scripture passage for each mystery. Tucked inside the pamphlet was a marker listing Mary's promises to Christians who pray the Rosary. I try now to pray the Rosary at the Grotto as often as possible. I have never had a prayer left unanswered when I have prayed at the Grotto.

ANONYMOUS
CLASS OF 1997

Freshman, senior, friend, alum
We come
With prayer for healthy and for sick
Lofting up on candle flame
From smoky wick
Silent tones amid the stones
Our Lady listens, comforts, comes.

PATRICK J. KENNEDY
CLASS OF 1967
BOULDER, COLORADO
DATED JULY 10, 1995

Patrick Kennedy died on December 30, 1995

VISITORS often leave flowers at the Grotto.

On October 4, 1985, two weeks after the fire, the following letter appeared in The Observer :

"I walked down to the Grotto the other night and was very pleased to find it virtually back to normal. That place has come to mean an awful lot to me in the four-plus years I've been here, and looking at its charred shell last week was quite hard to take. When I first came to Notre Dame, I didn't even know the Grotto existed. I stumbled on it by accident one day as I was walking around St. Mary's Lake. I was immediately impressed with its beauty and the peace it seemed to bring to everyone who stopped to pray. Within a month or two, the Grotto had become a pretty regular part of my life. I didn't go there every day but when I need a little lift or just a break a from the pressures of freshman year, the Grotto was always the first place to go. I can remember breaking up with my girlfriend from home that year. The night I realized things were finally over, I walked down to the Grotto and had a good cry. Being there did not make my problems go away, but it sure made me feel a lot more at peace with what had happened. Not too long after that, I had wandered down for a late-night prayer and there was a girl sitting on a bench, crying. After much hesitation, I sat down next to her and asked her what was wrong and if she'd like to talk about it. Since I had been in the same position myself, it just seemed to be the right thing to do. My Hawaiian roommate at the time, called it the Aloha Spirit. I do not know what it was, but I know there was something about being so close to God that made me want to help that girl, even though she was a total stranger.

Sophomore year I spent some of the worst moments of my life at the Grotto. One of my best friends was killed in an automobile accident and I was bitter and angry. I lit candles, knelt on the kneelers, sat on the benches, wandered around the grassy area between the Grotto and the lakes — all the while questioning God. I went there frequently after my friend died, mad at God every time. Yet even through my anger, I felt that when I was at the Grotto, God was near me and He was trying to make me understand what had happened. Slowly, after many nights of praying and questioning, and through the love and understanding of a very special friend, I was able to accept my friend's death. Even when I questioned God and my beliefs so severely, when I was at the Grotto I would never feel He had abandoned me.

Last year, the Grotto became more than just a convenient link to God, but a link to my days at Notre Dame as well. Just before graduation, when the seniors made their last trip to the Grotto, I carried a candle from Sacred Heart Church to the Grotto. I can still remember exactly where I placed my candle and exactly where my girlfriend placed hers, as well. Even though that candle holder is yet to be replaced because of the fire, that spot remains a link to my memories of the previous four years. It has made the Grotto a symbol of Notre Dame and all this place has come to mean to me and an expression of the beliefs that are so important to me. I guess if anything good could possibly have come from last week's fire, it is that I now appreciate the Grotto more and realize more fully the unique role it plays in my life and the lives of many others around campus.

MIKE WILKINS
CLASS OF 1985, 1988 J.D.
INDIANAPOLIS, INDIANA

THE GROTTO CAUGHT FIRE in the early morning hours of September 23, 1985, when an estimated 1,500 candles were lit the weekend of a home game against Michigan. The candle flames ignited their plastic holders. The late Brother Borromeo Malley, Notre Dame fire chief at the time, described it this way: "It was one hell of a fire. Heavy, black smoke belched from the Grotto. The heat was so intense that when water came in contact with the stone, it caused spalling, which happens when the stones become overheated and chip or fall off in blocks." Large pieces lay on the ground in front of the rocks. Evidence remains on the keystone, which is missing a corner. Now, a limited number of candles are allowed to burn and glass containers have replaced plastic ones.

In 1987, Coni Rich wrote an article for The Observer *about her father's visit for Junior Parents' Weekend. At their last visit to the Grotto that weekend, her father took off his Notre Dame ring from the Class of 1954. The ring had been ever-present on his finger throughout Coni's childhood as a symbol of his devotion to Notre Dame. He asked Coni to keep it with her, close to the Grotto, when he left to return home to Arizona, where Coni's mother battled cancer. His hope was that his wife would return for Coni's graduation and retrieve the ring.*

By the time the article was published, I had flown home to be with my mother for a few days, and during those days in Phoenix, I received over 2,000 letters, cards, telegrams, faxes, packages, amulets, rosaries ... we were completely overwhelmed with love and support from my Notre Dame family.

In October, I received a call that it was time to come home. At the end of that call, my mom said: "Coni Jo, bring your father's ring home with you. I know why he wanted you to keep it there. I know I'm supposed to get it on your graduation day, but, honey, I don't think I'm going to make it. Don't worry, though, I'll have the best seat in the house!" I'll never forget the look in Dad's eyes when Mom put the ring back on his finger. "I've never felt more peaceful," she said. "I'm ready now. You keep that ring on your finger where it belongs and I promise I'll be O.K." Mom died on November 12, 1987. I sat at the Grotto many nights afterwards, saying a little thank you that my beautiful, wonderful, bright, funny, lively, lovely, perfect mother died with dignity and peace and love and the knowledge that her story had touched so many.

I'm not in South Bend anymore. I moved away two years ago to come to work in New Jersey. For a time, I "visited" the Grotto every night in my prayers, and now, I go there when times are hard, the day gets too crazy, or I just need to remind myself who and what I am. I go there when I question why I'm here, what I'm doing, where I'm going, or where I've been. I go there for peace, and love, and clarity. I go to my Grotto for inspiration, for confirmation, and mostly for the stillness. I go to the Grotto when I'm happy, when I'm sad, when I'm bored and lonely, or when I have so much to share that I think my head will explode. No matter how muddled my thoughts when I take my seat on one of those benches, my head is never more firmly in place, nor my feet more firmly on the ground than when I stand up and take the walk down the path toward the lake or climb the steps to the little walkway behind Sacred Heart. The Grotto is the single most important place and influence in my life. My friends know that when I come to visit South Bend, our first stop will be my tearful walk up the pathway from the lake, and my goodbye will always take place under the protection of Mary's peaceful gaze.

I ask that the students at Notre Dame do all of us alums a favor. As you pass by the Grotto, please give it a little wink and prayer for those of us who can only carry it in our hearts. Ask the spirit of Notre Dame to find us and carry us through, and no matter our location, protect and strengthen us until we can be there again.

CONI RICH
CLASS OF 1989
MARGATE, NEW JERSEY

It was June 1968. Like many other nuns of that era, I was looking forward to spending another summer at Notre Dame — in my case, to complete my masters degree in communication arts. Even as I was packing, I detected a lump in my breast. It was malignant, and instead of enjoying the sights and sounds of summer on campus, I spent the time convalescing after a total radical mastectomy. Rather than returning to the stress and strain of my teaching duties in September, I was given a leave of absence to spend the fall semester at Notre Dame. During those precious months, I spent many hours at the Grotto praying for Our Lady's help for the future. Although I have since left religious life, I continue to cherish memories of Notre Dame and that special spot where all, repeat ALL, my prayers were answered.

ISOBEL PLANT 1969 M.A.
BRANTFORD, ONTARIO, CANADA

When we told our seven-year-old son, Nick, that we were going to Notre Dame for the weekend, he was excited to return to the place where we have had many fun family outings. Nick asked if we could go to "that place."
"Where? The bookstore?" "No."
"The Golden Dome?" "No."
"The ACC?" "No."
"Where?" "You know: That place."
"What place?" "God's Cave."
We knew immediately that he meant the Grotto. We took Nick to the Grotto on that trip and on every visit since. He still calls it God's Cave.

JIM TOMSHACK
PORTAGE, MICHIGAN

It was the beginning of finals week during my sophomore year and I had lit a candle with a prayer that everything would go all right and through God's will I wouldn't fail anything. Well, I finished with exams early, a Thursday morning, 9 a.m. to be exact, and I had the desire to return to the Grotto to give thanksgiving, relish in the feeling of being free of sophomore chains, and to pray for a successful junior year. I felt everything had gone well and after the rigorous semester it was great to think that all the hard work and long days had paid off. As I sat there upon the bench praying silently to myself, a runner came along and sat near me. After a moment or two we introduced ourselves and began talking. I learned that she was a student from Saint Mary's with a warm southern accent which was friendly enough to tell me of her plans of going overseas to study in Australia next semester and sadly that she stopped at the Grotto (like most runners do) for the special intention of asking for God's hand in her mother's upcoming cancer surgery. I asked if I may extend a prayer and she kindly accepted. Afterward, I tried to get her mind off her worries and we talked for a spell and during that time we had a visitor — a gentleman that I had never met until that moment. He seemed like he knew my new friend and spoke to her for a bit and then asked us both if we'd celebrate with him. He said: "I just took my last exam ever here and my parents sent me this bottle of champagne (which he took out of his blue duffel bag) to celebrate with. I don't drink much but I'd really like it if you'd have a drink with me." It was the most uncanny thing, but there I was sipping a glass of champagne with two complete strangers at the most wonderful place in the world. I toasted to his health and prosperity (it was the best I could think of at the time) and wished him well upon his future endeavors, which I believe he said would be the Air Force. I left the Grotto that day with the sense that it's one of the few places where people can meet as strangers and be moved to friendship through a common bond with God.

GARRETT MORASKI
CLASS OF 1997
NOTRE DAME, INDIANA

Rev. Thomas J. O'Donnell, C.S.C. '41 wrote in a 1963 Scholastic:

"The canopy of trees, digging their roots into the unhewn rock, is the proudest grove on campus. And rightly so.
These trees are a garland of green on a crown of rocks. They have lived up to all the beauty of Kilmer's poem ... as all trees must.
But these have done more. They have listened to May songs; they have watched flickering vigil lights; they have stood as silent
sentinels while anxious prayers and burdened hearts lifted hopeful eyes to Our Lady.
The trees of the Grotto — if they could speak — would speak only in a whisper ..."

> KINTZ and other neighboring farmers hauled great boulders from their land to Notre Dame — some weighing 2 to 3 tons. During construction of the Grotto, the boulders collapsed twice when timber supports built to hold the mortared boulders in place were removed.

My great-grandfather, Peter John Kintz II, came to South Bend in 1879. He purchased property just north of Notre Dame in order to farm. They were a very religious family and had great devotion to Mary. They would say the Rosary every night before retiring. We have often heard that great-grandfather hauled rocks from his farm specifically to be used for the Grotto.

My grandfather, John C. Kintz wanted more than farming had to offer so he went to Notre Dame and started to work as an apprentice carpenter. He was soon a full-fledged carpenter. One of his first big jobs was the carpentry work on the Dujarie Building. Peter John Kintz's oldest child, Clara Ann, joined the Holy Cross order in 1875 and was given the name Sister Mary Linus. The family still owns property just north of the toll road off Juniper Road on Kintz Road. My uncle, Elmer Kintz, was superintendent manager of construction of the Joyce Center. The Kintz family were members of Sacred Heart Parish from the time they moved to South Bend. The Kintz family has a long and wonderful heritage of which Notre Dame is a large part and we are proud of that fact.

MARY JO KINTZ SINEY
MISHAWAKA, INDIANA

My husband, Jerry Gillotti, is a ND graduate, Class of 1963. His brother, Gabriel Gillotti, graduated in 1959. In gratitude to their mother for helping her sons attend Notre Dame, a ND miniature was presented to her inscribed: "To Mom — GG '59, JG '63." Lucillie Gillotti passed away in April 1969, and Jerry gave his mom's ND miniature to me. Visiting the Grotto was always a must for Mom Gillotti and is now our family tradition. Over the years our teenage daughter, Ginny, has grown to love Notre Dame as much as her father. One autumn evening after attending a victorious football game and Mass at Sacred Heart Church, we journeyed toward the Grotto before leaving campus. There at the Lourdes Grotto, Jerry reminded us that prayers to Our Lady, especially during exams, was what got him through Notre Dame. He then told Ginny how the Grotto was a special place for a special lady, her grandmother. Amidst the glow of prayerful candles, father presented to daughter the Notre Dame miniature in honor of the grandmother she had never got to meet. The tradition continues.

KATHLEEN GILLOTTI
LAKE ZURICH, ILLINOIS

    We have visited the Grotto many, many times! Three years ago our six-year-old grandson, Michael, was to have a portion of his brain removed due to having a stroke at birth. Along with that, he had fluid on his brain and had to have a shunt put in behind his ear. Then came the seizures! It was a total nightmare. So to the Grotto we went, my husband and I, along with Michael and his nine-year-old sister, Heather. We all lit candles and prayed until we cried. After his arrival at Johns Hopkins, Dr. Freeman decided to put him on the Ketogenic diet. The diet lasted almost thirty-nine months. Since Christmas our daughter has been weaning him slowly to normal everyday food. We praise God and Mary very highly. You see, Michael will be ten years old soon; seizure-free; no surgery and off of all medication. He is a third grader at St. Jude's. In fact, when we picked up the grandkids today, I took time and lit a candle and talked to Mary. We have so much to be thankful for! We are forever grateful, especially when we visit the Grotto! Thanks.

GERTRUDE BOEMBEKE
MISHAWAKA, INDIANA

Jim McGuire graduated from Notre Dame with an undergraduate degree in 1936 and a law degree in 1938. During his six years at Notre Dame he visited the Grotto daily to pray to Our Lady. He always said that is how he succeeded at Notre Dame. From the time he left Notre Dame, he had the greatest desire to build his own grotto. Jim finally made his dream come true when we retired to Florida in the early 1970s. We collected rocks for months. As Florida has mainly soft, porous coquina, we completed our rock collection on a trip to our home town of Rochester, New York, and returned with a car full of rocks. Our grotto was build inside our screened-in porch. We started with a large baby's bath tub, lined it with concrete, and built up concrete and rocks around it until the grotto was about six feet tall. We purchased a pump and tubing to create a waterfall, and placed a statue of Mary into the Grotto to complete our special project.

For the next twenty years, sitting on our porch was peaceful, as we listened to the water trickle over our grotto of Notre Dame. We often said our Rosary sitting by the grotto. In 1980, Jim had his larynx removed in a cancer operation, and after that travel became difficult for him. After years of not visiting the Notre Dame campus, our son Jim, Jr. (ND Class of '65) helped us travel to the campus for the Northwestern football game in the fall of 1993. It was exciting because our grandson, Jim III (ND Class of '94) was a current student. Our first night in South Bend, Jim suffered severe heart pains and was rushed to the hospital where it was discovered he had angina and, also, fluid on the lung. Our family ended up watching the game with Jim in the hospital. When Jim was able to travel, Jim Jr. took us first to the campus where we visited the restored Sacred Heart Church and, of course, the Grotto. It was Jim's last visit to Notre Dame. He proudly talked on the telephone to our grandson, Jim III, on his graduation day in May 1994.

Our four sons and our daughter helped me plan a Notre Dame-theme funeral Mass. It was held at Queen of Peace Church in Rochester, where Jim was the first trustee and led the building of the church. Our son, Jim Jr., gave the eulogy, highlighting his father's devotion to Our Lady. Our oldest grandchild spoke on behalf of our fourteen grandchildren and some of the older grandchildren were pall bearers. The younger ones took up the gifts, which included a Notre Dame banner, Jim's favorite ND hat, and a family picture from our 50th anniversary celebration. The Mass was supported by hymns to Our Lady, including the Notre Dame Alma Mater and, at the end, Jim's casket was walked from the church to a moving, organ-rendition of the Notre Dame fight song. It was an appropriate tribute to a man who loved Our Lady and the University of Notre Dame so much.

Jim's days at Notre Dame, and his daily visits to the Grotto, formed the basis for our life-long devotion to the Mother Mary. She continues to give me strength, and I pray daily that Jim's devotion to Notre Dame will be continued through his family.

MRS. JAMES H. (GROVENE S.) MCGUIRE
WEBSTER, NEW YORK

AS PREFECT OF RELIGION for 16 years before being made University President in 1934, Rev. John F. O'Hara wrote religious bulletins that were put under students' doors to remind them to pray at the Grotto. In his June 1, 1925, bulletin Father O'Hara writes: "A year ago Ralph Adams Cram (who later designed the South Dining Hall) stated that the Grotto is the best piece of art at Notre Dame. Aside from its artistic value, many a student has found it the most inspiring place on the grounds. If you neglected it during the month of the Blessed Virgin, you still have a week in which to learn its beauties and its inspiration. Drop down there after Holy Communion: call again before you go to bed at night. Stand back far enough to see the dome and statue towering over it; then approach and kneel before the statue. The girlish figure in white built this school. On your knees thank the Blessed Virgin for Notre Dame. The old boys who amount to something want to visit the Grotto when they come back here; you will too in your own good time if you learn its secret while you are here."

Maybe it was the Blessed Mother that brought me to Notre Dame — I know it was she who kept me there. Graduating from St. Mary's elementary school in 1932, I next attended public high school in a city where Catholics were a minority group, and graduated in 1936. Depression years. No family money for college. Oldest of four. During two years of employment, I turned down a hockey scholarship and a fraternity job because the school did not have an engineering school. Also, I turned down an opportunity to attend both military academies. I wanted a pure engineering education, not military oriented. (I was only 17 out of high school. What did I know?) Enter a subway alumnus cousin of mine. He suggested Notre Dame. I said no way. Too expensive. Finally I did apply after an error was corrected in my high school grade information. Now I'm there. My next hurdle: to stay there. I needed a campus job, so I camped out under the Dome outside the administration offices until they got tired of seeing me. Result: a job as set-up man for breakfast in the West Dining Hall and a job working on the religious bulletin staff. The latter job required me to distribute the bulletin to every residential hall and other occupied building on campus five days a week. Between the two jobs it was necessary to pass by the Grotto at least once a day and sometimes twice or more. The Lady and I became good friends. She listened to all my problems: girl friend troubles, chemistry, thermo-dynamics, calculus and — oh yes, money! I never thought I'd finish. The source of each semester's tuition was up for grabs. The only constant was the Grotto and Our Lady. She always listened and together we made it. Fifteen years later I made the last payment.

During those four years of visiting the Grotto I began to wonder what the original Grotto was really like ... so much wondering that I wanted to visit and see firsthand. My wonderful wife agreed, and we made the journey in 1990. It was an unbelievable experience. The similarity in the physical appearance of the two Grottos is incredible. The other surprise was the number and mix of people. For two days we watched and prayed — the handicapped, the infirmed on gurneys, in wheel chairs, crutches, rosaries being said, outside confessionals set up for every language, the beautiful church. We saw it all and came away with the same sense of serenity that I left with each visit to the Grotto at Notre Dame du Lac. (The Lady and I still talk a lot about the eight children and eighteen grandchildren among other things — including ND football).

JOSEPH A. RORICK
CLASS OF 1942
VERO BEACH, FLORIDA

When I reflect on my Notre Dame experience, I remember the wonderful times with my lifelong friends and the late nights (or early mornings) at the Grotto. It did not matter how far below zero the mercury dropped or how many academic obligations I was juggling. I always ended my day at the Grotto. Before I left my "dome home" (Breen Phillips) I checked in with my friends to inquire about special intentions. Many times someone would offer to join me on my Grotto trip. We would take the path which ran along the side of Zahm, under the covered entrance of St. Ed's and through the dark tunnel of the Administration Building. Once there, we basked in the glow of the lighted candles and the lamplights, and offered our silent prayers. At the Grotto, I could feel the connectedness of the Notre Dame community, as I shared the kneeler with as many as a dozen other students each night. It was there that I cultivated my deeper understanding of God, myself, and my relationships at Notre Dame and at home in New Jersey and Pennsylvania.

MARY EILEEN (KENNEY) BALTES
CLASS OF 1986
DOYLESTOWN, PENNSYLVANIA

In August of 1991, after being married and childless for ten years, my eldest son Joseph and his wife Debra decided to begin the process of getting qualified as prospective adoptive parents in New York State. They received little encouragement and were told that they would have to wait a minimum of five years and as long as seven to ten years to obtain a baby. On October 31 of that year I turned sixty and as a birthday present my wife, Angela, arranged for us to go to Notre Dame for a football weekend. We flew from New York to Indiana and, as has been my custom whenever I visit the campus, the first thing I did was to go straight to the Grotto to tell Mother I was home. I lit a candle and asked our Blessed Mother to help Joey and Debbie in their quest for a baby and to perhaps speed up the process a little bit. When we arrived home in New York from Indiana, exactly a week from the time I lit the candle at the Grotto — in fact, exactly to the hour — I got a call from Joey. He said "Dad, I've got great news. We have a baby for adoption except there is only one complication. We have to go to Indiana to get the baby."

I am convinced that the Indiana part was thrown in by Our Lady of the Grotto to make sure I recognized that it was through her intercession that my prayer was answered. Our fifth grandson, Nicholas, was born on November 12, 1991, four months after Joey and Debbie started the adoption process and is our beautiful gift from God who came into our family through the intercession of our Blessed Mother.

MANEUL A. SEQUEIRA, JR.
CLASS OF 1954
CROSS RIVER, NEW YORK

"Layer by layer, like Jerusalem, the Grotto continues to be sanctified by the laughter, prayers, and faith that binds us as Christians and members of the University community. 'It is the light within us that draws us to Notre Dame,' believes Father Bob Krieg. And apparently, this light is best nourished at the Grotto, where its solitude, beauty and holiness will magnetize students for another hundred years."

— from an essay partially published in The Observer, *February 15, 1996, by Laura Merritt, Class of 1996*

I am a 1988 grad of Notre Dame and in my senior year part of my Lenten commitment was to attend Mass at least twice a week. I broke that commitment one week when I opted not to attend Sunday night Mass in Alumni Hall, but instead I watched a movie with some friends. Feeling guilty about my actions, I decided that I would redeem myself by spending the same amount of time at the Grotto that I would have spent at Mass that night. At around midnight I headed for the Grotto. It was a beautiful night — calm and rather serene. As I knelt down to pray at the Grotto, I felt pretty good about my decision to spend this time. Then I felt the first raindrop, then the second, third ... and before long it was pouring rain. As I watched others at the Grotto run for cover, my first thought was to do the same. I thought, however, that maybe God was testing my true resolve to make up for breaking my Lenten promise. So, I knelt and prayed alone in one of the most severe thunderstorms I had ever seen for forty-five minutes. I got up to leave the Grotto and my clothes were drenched. I headed back to Alumni Hall. As I got to the South Quad the rain started to let up and by the time I arrived at Alumni Hall, it had stopped. Thankfully, not many people were still awake when I returned to my dorm, and I didn't need to explain my appearance to anyone. I hesitate to say that my experience that night was a message from God, but it was surely an enriching moment in my life.

May the Grotto always live on as the centerpiece of Notre Dame's great campus.

DANIEL R. FRITZ
CLASS OF 1988
SIOUX FALLS, SOUTH DAKOTA

For years, as a student, I worked evenings and nights for Notre Dame Security. It was not uncommon that I got off work at one or two a.m. and yet, at those hours, even in feet of snow, when I would stop by the Grotto enroute back to the dorm, I would find someone there praying. Whatever the time or occasion, we had the Grotto.

REX REMPEL
CLASS OF 1993
SEATTLE, WASHINGTON

My story really begins on January 1st, 1991. At halftime of the Cotton Bowl, I bought some flowers, drove to Notre Dame, wrote a letter to the Blessed Mother consecrating my life to her guidance, and left it at the base of the Grotto. That moment changed my life. When it was time to marry the woman to whom the Blessed Mother had led me, there was no doubt in my mind where I would propose.

It was late February. We were living in Arizona and had flown back to visit my family in Elkhart. One evening we went to see Fr. Heppen in Corby Hall. After our visit, he excused himself to keep an appointment and Margy and I walked down to the Grotto. As my best friend Craig and my brothers looked on from the pine trees, we lit a candle, said a prayer, then sat down on a bench. At my signal (putting my arm around Margy), a few men began singing and walking towards us on the bench. They were the Notre Dame Glee Club in disguise. As they continued, Margy realized that everyone at the Grotto that night could sing. Eventually there were 10 Glee Clubbers standing in a semi-circle singing a lively love song to Margy after they had laid long stem roses on her lap. They sang a verse of a very soft, beautiful tune, then began humming as I knelt down, produced the ring and made my request. She said yes. Perfectly on key, the Glee Club chimed in again.

After one more song, a hymn in honor of the Virgin Mary (the Alma Mater), Margy's serenaders marched into the winter night, a spirited rendition of the Victory March on their lips. Emotionally over-whelmed while walking back across campus, we passed the Log Cabin Chapel and I told Margy to look inside. The door flung open as she approached. Looking squarely at her from inside were her parents who had secretly flown in from Arizona, her siblings who had driven from Columbus, Ohio, my parents, my twelve siblings, their families and a few friends who had come in for the occasion. As the children watched in quiet awe, the Glee Club sang their songs again for the benefit of those who had not viewed the event from the evergreen gallery. Presently, Fr. Heppen emerged, fully vested for Holy Mass, keeping the commitment he had mentioned earlier. And everyone prayed. When Mass was over, I had reserved the upper room at Bruno's Pizza. The rest of the night was passed in festive celebration.

Only afterwards did I realize the enormity of the weekend. Margy and I were going to be married. Our Lady's guidance had once again prevailed.

BOBBY KLOSKA
CLASS OF 1990
SCOTTSDALE, ARIZONA

Going to college was not my plan. It was a result of a deathbed promise to my mother during my senior year of high school. Kind teachers helped me prepare for entrance exams and take additional courses during the summer after graduation to help meet requirements. Also, Notre Dame allowed me to take some language courses to apply towards admittance, and not my degree. As you can see, I was poorly prepared and very surprised at being admitted. That first year was very hard for me, and almost my last.

During the course of the year, 1956, I had come to know the Grotto, but wasn't much of a believer in prayer as my prayers for my mother had seemed to have been ignored. I shared a large first floor room in Zahm Hall with two other young men from New York State. It was next to an entranceway and as a result, somewhat noisy. My fellow students had come from better school systems, and were prepared. Passing grades were not so easy for me to obtain.

At that time the school believed in forcing the students to get needed rest and would shut off the main power so that study lamps, electric clocks, water pumps, etc. would not work. My roommates were studying to be electrical engineers, and they knew a lot about electricity and decided to re-wire the room so they could study later. They removed the mirrored cabinet above our sink to gain access to the needed wires, and we found a number of photographs left by previous students. We removed them and added some of our own, along with the current student publications, I believe. The new lighting worked for awhile, but upon return from vacation, it was discovered that unknown persons had restored the original wiring, replastered and repainted. The photos reflected a previous student's interest in football and in acting youthful and somewhat silly, and his strong attachment to Our Lady and the Grotto. The pictures appeared old to me even back then, but the Grotto seemed ageless. I became fascinated with the fact that my predecessor had obviously frequented the Grotto, and began to make this a nightly habit also. Prayer again became important to me, not so much for myself, but to seek the help to complete that promise to my mother. I worked hard, harder than most it seemed to me, just to stay in school, and I know it wouldn't have been enough without the many blessings which came my way via the Grotto.

To this day, I have a small grotto beneath a waterfall in my back yard and frequently say a prayer for current students; that they too might find and use this source of peace and guidance. Great wealth was never a goal of mine, but good health and contentment and a chance to be of help to others was, and I believe those four years at the Grotto helped me achieve not only my promise, but those as well.

GERALD E. LEPPEK
CHICAGO, ILLINOIS

In May of 1992, I had the fortune to attend the National Medjugorje Conference at the University of Notre Dame. On the first evening of the Conference the attendees have a candlelight Rosary walk to the Grotto. It is by far the most beautiful sight ever seen. On this occasion, however, as I approached the Grotto — in heels nonetheless — I was again fortunate to be one of maybe several hundred to find an empty chair to sit on, I among thousands of people. As I sat contemplating the Rosary, the woman next to me asked if I was wearing perfume, which I was not. She then started to cry prompting me to ask if I could help her. She answered, "Can't you smell it?" I, not knowing what "it" was said no, I did not smell anything — at least at that instant I did not because only several seconds (maybe 30) later I was given the grace of smelling the most beautiful scent of oil of rose. It lasted maybe several minutes and was gone as quickly as it had come. None of the people sitting around us had moved during that time, all were still sitting in their same spots. Our Lady was present to me and wanted me to know She was there. What a great gift She had given me! This was the first time I was allowed to know of Her presence. It has subsequently happened at other times, most notably while I was praying in St. James Church in Medjugorje last September, 1994.

Praise be to Jesus and Mary! I am reluctant to use my name so I'll just sign it —

CHILD OF OUR LADY

It was August, 1938. I was a patient at Healthwin Hospital, then the county TB sanitarium. It is four miles northwest of Notre Dame on a bluff above the St. Joseph River. The lakes at Notre Dame drain into the St. Joseph. The river is a half-mile to the west and fifty feet lower than the lakes. On a pleasant summer evening early in the month, we patients were resting quietly in our beds on a screened-in porch that faced south. I began to hear singing — men's voices coming from a distance and barely audible. I listened attentively. The melody sounded familiar. Yes, yes, it was the hymn for Benediction, "Down in Adoration Falling." But where could it be coming from? Then I remembered the annual retreat for laymen was going on at Notre Dame. The retreatants, several hundred of them, were assembled for the evening conference and benediction at the Grotto. What a benediction for me that Grotto singing was!

GEORGE SCHIDEL, C.S.C.
CLASS OF 1934, 1952 M.A.
NOTRE DAME, INDIANA

I was a doctoral student at the University of Notre Dame from 1964 to 1969. Each step toward final completion of the degree was a distinct challenge. The written and oral examinations taken upon completion of most required course work was perhaps the most challenging step. Each step, of course, was accompanied by many visits to the Grotto. On the morning after the successful completion of my written and oral exams, I hurried to the Grotto to engage in prayers of thanksgiving. In the midst of my praying a voice that came from behind me said, "So Our Lady came through for you, huh?" I turned and saw a Catholic priest I did not know and have never seen since. Smiling I said, "She sure did, Father." He smiled back and walked away.

FRANK A. STANCATO
1969 PH.D.
MOUNT PLEASANT, MICHIGAN

As a resident of St. Ed's during my years at Notre Dame, many were the nights that I would walk out into the midnight-cold air, past the back door of the Administration Building and down to the Grotto, the snow crunching beneath my feet. Seldom would I find myself alone: almost always someone would be kneeling, or there would be fresh footprints in the snow. Many years and a few continents later, it remains the place I feel closest to the Lord.

Twelve years after I graduated, I would be engaged there. More recently, it has taken on another meaning. When my wife and I initiated steps to adopt from China, the first thing we did was to ask Father Scully to light a candle for the daughter whom we had yet to meet but whom I was sure had already been born. I learned that the Notre Dame family is no abstraction: others who walked down the Grotto steps to light candles for us include Bill Sexton and Steve Grissom in Admissions. Steve's, in particular, means a great deal to us because he is a Presbyterian and it is a most an-Presbyterian thing to do.

Our daughter's name is Grace, and when we received our notice from China they listed her birthday as July 11, 1995. We went back and checked the date we filled out the initial application form (which we did the very first day after we made our decision): that date was July 12. We reached our decision the day she was born. It is not a particularly extraordinary story, but it is very, very real and — for that reason — for us, very, very special. The next candle we light at the Grotto will be this summer, for a prayer heard. And Grace will be there watching.

WILLIAM MCGURN
CLASS OF 1980
HONG KONG

I recall vividly, though it occurred well over 40 years ago, when as a teenaged freshman I first stopped at the Grotto on the way back to St. Edwards — my dormitory — from the Dining Hall. While the Grotto is particularly lovely and serene in the snow, my first views of it in 1950 were with its craggy surfaces outlined in the special radiance of the late summer sun reflecting off the dappled surface of St. Mary's Lake. I recall stopping at the Grotto at first as much out of curiosity, all of us freshmen having heard a great deal about it as a campus landmark and as a piece of Notre Dame history, as I did out of any need to communicate with Our Lady or to be comforted by her.

However, as the pressures of collegiate life started to build that autumn and the waves of homesickness and loneliness washed over me, I found that my nightly visits to the Grotto went beyond the curious and into the necessary. So, what began as a tangential element of my walk back to St. Ed's after dinner became a very important, almost indispensable, part of my student day.

Then, more readily than I would have expected, the autumn of 1950 stretched into weeks and then months and then years. All of a sudden, I was a senior at Notre Dame and, soon thereafter, I was an alumnus living and working thousands of miles away from "That Special Place," as Father Hesburgh so beautifully terms the campus. But visits to the Grotto remain as important to me in my sixth decade of life as when I was a teenager. Upon return visits to the campus, which are less frequent than I would wish, I always make a point to visit the Grotto. But reflecting the changes brought by the intervening years, my prayers at the Grotto are no longer to pass the history exam or the accounting final, but for the well-being of my family, for the health of surviving classmates and for the repose of those friends who have passed beyond.

So, in celebrating the centennial of the Grotto, we celebrate both the fragility and the flux of life, which the Grotto has witnessed these past 100 years, as well as the stability and the continuity of life which it also has witnessed during this century. I am happy that it was there for students of early eras when they needed it. And, I pray it will be there for another hundred years to repair and to enrich the lives of future generations.

ROMANO L. MAZZOLI
CLASS OF 1954
LOUISVILLE, KENTUCKY

Hon. Romano L. Mazzoli retired in January, 1995, after 24 years as U.S. Representative to Kentucky's 3rd Congressional District. The federal office building in Louisville has been named after him.

It began in 1973. We brought our son to Notre Dame to attend the University. A tour of the campus led us to the Grotto. There, we lit candles for various intentions and, without realizing it, started a tradition that has endured ever since. On visits thereafter, we would always stop at the Grotto and light candles. Then in 1979, Anne, my wife was diagnosed as having lymphoma. So, from that point on we tried to keep a candle burning for her at the Grotto. Any time one of us were there we always went to the Grotto first, to pray and light a candle.

It was Anne's wish that she would have enough time to see our youngest child raised and settled. Chris was 14 at that time. We feel her prayers were answered because when she died on October 15, 1988 he was almost 23 and about to be married. It has been almost eight years since she died and I cherish my visits there now more than ever because when I light a candle in the Grotto, it brings back so many sweet memories. Any time one of our children are there, they do the same. And now even our grandchildren are carrying on the tradition.

ANTHONY PARILLO
GIRARD, OHIO

I have been fortunate to be able to organize bus trips to see the Irish play since 1988. On October 2, 1994, we attended the Stanford game. I had a special lady along — Margie O'Donnell. It was her first time ever to Notre Dame. She was 64 years old and had previously been to Ireland.

I caught up with her at the Grotto while roaming the campus and there she told me that her trip to Notre Dame was better than her trip to Ireland. And she wanted to come again the next year. Unfortunately, she suffered a heart attack on November 20th and passed away. The 1995 trip on September 1 was dedicated in Margie's honor, with Margie's three children along. I asked Michael, Francis, and Peggy Sue to meet me and our group of about 20 at the Grotto to light a candle for their mother. There, we presented them with rosaries that had been blessed by Father Malloy. This was a very emotional moment. I had lost my own parents one day apart in May of 1994. My mother died at my father's wake. It was the most unbelievable circumstance. My brother and I buried both our parents on the same day. I think this type of situation is why the Grotto was made.

JACK KMETZ
JIM THORPE, PENNSYLVANIA

I am blessed to be a freshman at Saint Mary's College in the Grotto's centennial year. Were it not for this quietly glowing haven carved from a campus that already seems to have been dropped from heaven, I may not be here at all. I asked my dorm hostesses to take me to the Grotto when they walked me "across the street" during my first campus visit to Saint Mary's. It was one of those crackling sharp autumn nights in South Bend when the football season is brand new, careful note taking in classes hasn't yet degenerated into mid-semester scrawl, and expectations float on air like the leaves swirling in the lamplight. The tangible uniqueness of the place was slowly seeping into my heart. I hadn't expected it to. I was a senior in a high school that I very much regretted leaving, and doubts about abandoning my home for the past eighteen years crowded my mind. The Grotto gently cleared them. As my hostesses and I approached, our conversation fell away. Without a word, we approached the single iron railing, me pleasantly stunned at the idea of four Generation Xers pausing to pray. The cold iron bit into the sleeves of my windbreaker as I knelt, but all I felt in my soul was the warm presence of Our Lady. Tears blurred the flickering candles into a soft gold haze as I heard God whisper to my heart, "You have found a home." He was right. Two weeks later my application as a candidate for Early Decision to Saint Mary's was in the mail. Ten months later I had moved on campus and into the lives of some of the most fantastic people I have ever met. And now, whether fighting my way past the eight-alum-deep crowds for a rapid petition on mornings of football Saturdays, or kneeling for a Rosary with the whole blessed place to myself as the morning sun begins to light the Dome above it, the Grotto anchors my soul as I rejoice in my days as a member of the Saint Mary's/Notre Dame community.

Kudos to Father Sorin for giving generations a peaceful home for the collegiate heart!

MARY BETH ELLIS
SMC CLASS OF 1999
NOTRE DAME, INDIANA

Father Edward Sorin prayed at an earlier shrine to Our Lady, built in 1878. It stood between the present Grotto and the church. An 1892 article titled: "Presbytery Gardens and Grounds" describes "a facsimile representation of the Grotto of Lourdes, beautifully sculptured out of the side of the declivity. The rocks are there portrayed, while underneath is the gurgling fountain. To one side, lifted on high, is a beautiful statue of Our Lady of the Immaculate Conception, encased in an octagonal frame, the sides of which are glass, supported by stone pillars. At a little distance is the kneeling figure of Bernadette. The statues were removed and placed in the new Grotto upon its dedication on the Feast of Our Lady of Snows, August 5, 1896, the same day that Father Sorin left France for the New World in 1841. The dedication brought five hundred or more priests, brothers and nuns of the Holy Cross assembled for morning Mass. Afterward, they processed to the Grotto, the brothers carrying the statue in the lead, while the others followed holding candles and waving banners. The nuns chanted the Litany of Loretto and the Magnificat. The statue was blessed and a sermon was given by Rev. William Corby, who was Provincial at that time.

THE EARLIEST known photograph of the Grotto, August, 1896
Rev. William Corby, C.S.C., is believed to be the priest kneeling
on the right at the railing.

I wish to add these anecdotes of the lore and the lure of the Grotto at Notre Dame. I was born and reared in South Bend at 1004 E. St. Vincent St. — within sight of the Golden Dome. Since the days I was able to walk, then ride a bike out to the campus, it always included a visit to the Grotto — to touch a stone from the Grotto at Lourdes imbedded in the wall, then light a candle to help send my prayers heavenward.

I was one of six sons of Thomas L. and Kathryn B. Hickey, who graduated from Notre Dame. Most often after class, before walking home, a visit was made to the Grotto. In June, 1944, as a Naval officer before leaving for duty at N.A.S. Pearl Harbor, my then fiance, Mary Hennigan (now my wife of 50 years) came from Boston for a "bon voyage" visit. We made daily visits to the Grotto imploring Our Lady's blessings for our future well-being and happiness. She didn't fail us. She heard our petitions.

On my first day back from the Pacific Theater in 1946, my Mary was waiting for me at my parents' home. Our first mission was a visit to the Grotto the next day to give thanks and to ask Our Lady's protection as we approached our wedding in September, 1946. My Mary and I placed our marriage in the protective hands of Mary, the Mother of God. We were blessed with five children. On our visits to my parents in South Bend from New England, my wife and I always brought the children out to the campus — and a visit to the Grotto — to allow them to absorb its sacred majesty. Soon they would ask us, "When can we visit the Grotto?"

We then knew of its lure.

Later, our three sons enrolled and graduated with honors from Notre Dame. Still later, after marriage, they would bring their families for visits to Notre Dame — and pilgrimages down to the Grotto, so their children would be imbued with its awesomeness.

In July 1994 our son, Brian, moved from Plano, Texas, to New Jersey. His wife flew with their daughter. Brian drove with the two sons, Brian, Jr. and Justin. They left Texas morning at 8 a.m. and drove through to Notre Dame's Morris Inn, arriving at 1 a.m. The boys had asked their dad if they could get a reservation on campus. Before going to bed and after driving for 16 hours, the boys said that they would like to first walk down for a visit at the Grotto. My son, and my wife and I also, were awed by this scene of their walking along the paths on a warm, full moon night — seeing the Golden Dome lighted brightly and then arriving at their peaceful sanctuary of the Grotto, all ablaze with burning candles. They had come back to their home away from home, asking for Our Lady's protection and blessings for themselves and their family, as they headed east to their new home and new friends.

This is a story that I needed to relate. The visit at 1 a.m. on that July night by the two boys with their father has been a source of pride and inspiration for my Mary and me — sensing that Our Lady continues to love us and will protect our family and ourselves all the days of our lives.

JOHN HICKEY
CLASS OF 1944, 1947
DOVER, MASSACHUSETTS

"I still feel a mounting exhilaration as I'm approaching the Grotto. I feel I am about to come in the presence of Our Lady. Nothing has changed. I've been to Tepeyac in Mexico City several times, where Our Lady actually appeared, and I don't feel that same sensation.

Maybe it's because as students here at a very crucial, tender, and decisive time in our lives, we shared our hopes, our struggles, our fears and our dreams with Our Lady at the Grotto. This is the great treasure that Notre Dame men and women have that none of the other great Universities can give. The Grotto became a living thing for us — a very personal communication. It was so more than 40 years ago for me, and it is so today. Nothing, nothing has changed."

JOSE GONZALEZ
CLASS OF 1950
LAREDO, TEXAS
SPOKEN APRIL 21, 1992, IN ACCEPTANCE OF AN AWARD FROM THE COLLEGE OF ENGINEERING

As an incoming freshman in 1965, I soon learned of the significance of the Grotto. I made the usual visits to pray for success in school, and for the well-being of my family, but I had special prayers for my 12-year-old brother, Bob.

Bob had been fighting cancer for five years. He seemed to be doing well, but my Aunt Emma died from cancer during Thanksgiving weekend of my freshman year. Many prayers were said for Bob, and they have been answered. Today he is the proud father of three children, and they are the best Notre Dame fans in the world. Bob visits Notre Dame often, and always makes a special visit to the Grotto. We are forever grateful for Notre Dame and the Grotto, and pray that the next 100 years bring continued hope and inspiration to all who visit both.

RON VERO
CLASS OF 1969
ALBANY, NEW YORK

This is a simple story. I am sure there are thousands before me who felt the same strength as I the day I left my daughter to begin her freshman year at Our Lady's University. I said a hurried goodbye, and then tried to be strong, and headed for the Snite Museum. Too many emotions were inside me, so I knew I would gain the peace I needed over at the Grotto. So there I walked, thinking so many thoughts as my child was quickly engulfed into a new beginning she was so anxious to partake in. I lit the biggest candle I could find, for our entire family, but mostly for the child who would live on the grounds I was about to vacate. I sat before Our Blessed Mother and thanked her for answering my prayers ... that my little girl would choose a college where her faith would continue to grow and where the good example of all the other Catholics there would only reinforce my little girl's faith.

Even though I felt tears streaming down my cheeks, and felt a separation sadness coming on, I felt an inner peace go through me that enabled me to walk away from the Grotto a stronger Mom than when I first sat before Mary. I tried not to cry, but knew that wouldn't work. A row or two behind me there was one other person, a woman, and she was crying, too. I felt a silent bond, for both of us, I was sure, were going through the same memories, feelings, longings, and milestones together, yet separately. I had spent almost a full week with my beautiful child, who was named a Notre Dame Scholar and earned herself her own place in this most wonderful University, and we bonded more so during that time than in a long, long time.

Before I left the Grotto I said a complete Rosary, which I had not touched for a long many years and it felt good. My journey home was through such turbulent skies in a violent thunderstorm, but on the airplane, I felt at peace. The young sailor next to me cried out, "Oh, my God!" and had his rosary in his hands and was very, very scared — as were all the passengers. But thanks to Our Mother and the strength I just had taken on, I had no fear at all. She certainly prepared me, not only for that long journey home, but for the remainder of my journey here on Earth.

SUZANNE M. GALLAGHER
WINTER PARK, FLORIDA

Indeed, the Grotto at Notre Dame has a special meaning to me.

During the late '50s, this growing teenager had a special bond with his immigrant Polish grandmother, Helen Cackowski. She was a special person in my life, and now that I was able to drive, it was "payback" time

for me. Neither of my grandparents ever had a driver's license, so I was more than happy to take them anywhere they asked. They seldom asked except for short trips to the market and grocery stores. My grandmother did have a special request whenever her time would permit. She would ask in her half English, half Polish accent, "Frenk ... you take me Grotto? Please?" I would never refuse her. She always dressed for the occasion. While making the long walk across campus, I could see her excitement. She loved to visit the Grotto. She told me once, "I talk to God. He a good man!" Sometimes her "talks" would last a little too long for me, so I would wander around campus, visit the log chapel and other familiar places. Upon my return to the Grotto, I would take a back seat in the last row of metal folding chairs always available for visitors and various services held at the Grotto. She would always join me when finished with her prayers and we would talk about anything that came to her mind. I remember those talks more than anything. She would pour her heart out to me on just about any matter on her mind. When we would get ready to leave she would give me a hug and thank me for bringing her and listening. Oh, how I miss those hugs! They were so very, very special. I graduated from high school in 1961, and she made trips to the Grotto a regular routine that summer. Our talks were also very special to her, too, and she knew I'd be going off to college, and her trips to the Grotto would be limited to the summer months and my visits home.

Grandma Cackowski died my sophomore year in college, and I was devastated. The pain of her loss left a scar on my heart that I find difficult to write about even on this day. Even today in my mid '50s the Grotto is a special place for me. I visit there regularly to reflect, pray and, of course, to have one of my talks with grandma. I get as excited as she did when entering the Grotto proper.

I thank the Notre Dame Alumni Association for giving me the opportunity to share this brief personal and sentimental anecdote with them on this 100th Anniversary of the Grotto. I've enclosed a 1961 photo of Grandma Cackowski with a background etched in my heart forever.

FRANK CACKOWSKI
MISHAWAKA, INDIANA

In 1983, the oldest of our five children was admitted to (and accepted) membership in the class of 1987 at Notre Dame. We encouraged her to go. Her dad was a graduate. She would love it! In August 1983 we drove the one hour to our airport in Albuquerque and put her on the plane. There was a huge lump in my throat. She was going to a foreign country, she was entering mainstream America. Could she adapt? Her entire childhood was different from anything we, her parents, had experienced growing up on the east coast. Maybe we were expecting too much. The excitement of the early weeks was exhilarating. She had made a good decision. Then, in October, it all seemed to fall apart. Professor Emil Hofman's letters to the freshman parents were poignant and scary. Essentially, he said homesickness was about to set in. How could this happen? Believe me, it happened. Our little girl called home distraught. There was not a chile or a tortilla or salsa or enchilada to be had for two hundred square miles. How could this be?

The long and the short of it is that she "lost it." One very lonesome night in October, she dried the tears, and took a walk to the Grotto. She was feeling more alone than at any time in her life. She lit a candle, and asked God for his help and guidance as she faced one of the toughest times in her young life. As she stood up to walk back to her dorm, a priest who happened to be there, started to walk beside her and engaged in conversation. "How are you doing? ... Is everything all right? ... I know it's tough to be so far away from home, but you really will do all right ... Every freshman feels the way you do tonight ... You are really trying to do a difficult thing, leaving home and living in a new place ... God will help you do this ... and I am available for you to talk to anytime ... You can do this.

Father Hesburgh was "working" the Grotto, as he was so wont to do. But this time he had no way of knowing the impact of what he was doing.

Yes, Johanna finished at Notre Dame, and went on to medical school. In June, 1995, she finished her residency in pediatrics at the University of New Mexico Medical Center and moved on to her "real job" — a physician in the Young Children's Health Clinic in the barrio of south Albuquerque where she will treat our state's most disadvantaged children. She will be speaking mostly in Spanish to parents who need her greatly. She will also be a junior faculty member at the University of New Mexico School of Medicine. And this would be enough, wouldn't it? But Johanna's successes also empowered her siblings to consider Notre Dame. Her three brothers also graduated from Notre Dame. One is a resident in ENT surgery, one is a candidate for a Ph.D. in theology, and one is a candidate for a Juris Doctor in Law.

... all because a humble priest saw a pained, lonesome freshman who needed a kind word. And so the Grotto is not a special place in and of itself, or a special place because of what has happened there. But it is a special place because of what can happen there ... in the past, and especially in the future.

RUTH D. KELLY
SANTA FE, NEW MEXICO

My most vivid memory of Notre Dame's Grotto is also my first memory of the Grotto, from the fall of 1972. I still remember as if it was yesterday the way the Grotto looked on that beautiful fall day.

During freshmen orientation weekend, Father Hesburgh celebrated Mass at the Grotto for the new women students. Even though I had attended Catholic schools from first grade through twelfth grade, and attended the many, many Masses that went with the Catholic education, I had never attended Mass outside. To look up through the trees that grew on top of and on the sides of the Grotto at the beautiful blue sky was amazing to me. To this day when I visit the Grotto, I look up to the sky and remember that first time I visited there.

That was the best introduction to Notre Dame my family and I could have been given. It seemed so natural that Father Hesburgh be there to welcome us to Notre Dame. And what a beautiful place to do it from!

BETSY KALL BROSNAN
CLASS OF 1976
NAPERVILLE, ILLINOIS

"I really believe that Our Lady watches over this place. I feel I ought to stop in and say thanks, and also pray that she keeps watching over it. I usually get down there in the wee hours of the morning when I leave the office. There is almost always someone down there ... rain, sleet, or snow. Every university has a place where students hang out for their social life, libraries where they study, and fields where they play sports. But how many have a praying place?"

Then-President Rev. Theodore Hesburgh, C.S.C., from The Observer, *February 13, 1986*

HOW *Grotto Stories* CAME TO BE ...

I am indebted in this project to the dedication, spirituality, and trust of Mrs. Dorothy Corson. Her four years of research into the history of the Grotto honors its centennial and the labors of her father, William Buckles, who built a replica of the Notre Dame Grotto on the grounds of St. Stanislaus Church in South Bend.

Dorothy and I see our own Grotto experience as something of a miracle. We first met when I worked in the Local History Room of the St. Joseph County Public Library. I was intrigued by the subject of her research and inspired by her perseverance.

In the fall of 1994, Dorothy brought her work to the attention of Elaine Cripe, editor of Alumni Publications, and asked if a request for personal stories relating to the Grotto could be placed in The *ALUMNI* Newsletter. Not long after hiring me as her assistant in March, Elaine gave me the assignment of writing the request for stories about the Grotto for the May 1995 issue of *ALUMNI*. I called Dorothy and said "You'll never guess where I'm working now and why I'm calling you." As the project evolved, Dorothy needed someone to adopt it. She says I was "planted in her path." Often when a question arose that seemed an obstacle in our path, Dorothy would say: "We'll just have to leave it up to Our Lady." During dry stretches in her research, Dorothy's prayer at the Grotto was: "Lady dressed in light, show me the way."

Rev. Thomas McAvoy, C.S.C., former University Archivist and historian once said: "To have a history is to have a name, and the richer the history the more glorious the name." The more Dorothy dug up the historical facts of the Grotto's first hundred years, the more she realized that it's the faith, the feelings, the stories of the people who visit there that is the true history and glory of the Grotto. And she wished for such stories to eventually accompany her manuscript in the University Archives. Here, I mingle the stories with some of Dorothy's findings from countless hours of perusing archival documents and unindexed campus publications.

On behalf of the readers who find inspiration in *Grotto Stories*, I thank the authors for their part in spreading the glory. I sensed great appreciation for the invitation to put their feelings into words. Months after writing her poignant Grotto remembrance, Mary Murphy said in a telephone conversation: "It was so good for me to reflect and make heads and tails of the experience." Expressing it in writing helped to make it a "learning moment," she said.

My life and the lives of those around me have certainly been enriched — not only in collecting the Grotto letters, but also by the personal notes that came later. Upon learning of the project many of the letter authors sent words of encouragement. Kathy Ferrone wrote: "Behind your work is another Mary. It was for her that the Grotto was built, so she will probably show the interest she has in your project in some amazing ways ... In your work, you are not alone. Expect many blessings as you watch things fall in place before you."

You were right, Kathy.

Thank you all.

MPDB